A Vineyard Rebirth

The Vineyard Sunset Series

Katie Winters

ALL RIGHTS RESERVED. No part of this publication may be reproduced, distributed, or transmitted in any form or by any means, including photocopying, recording, or other electronic or mechanical methods, without the prior written permission of the publisher.

Copyright © 2021 by Katie Winters

This is a work of fiction. Any resemblance of characters to actual persons, living or dead is purely coincidental. Katie Winters holds exclusive rights to this work. Unauthorized duplication is prohibited.

Chapter One

The ragged edge of the cliffside thrilled her. Marilyn left her shoes at the rock just behind her and curved her toes just at the brink of the bluff— where, if she teetered just the slightest bit forward, she would be cast forth to the wild seas below. It was September, and Marilyn had been married to James Peterson for only two months. The "I do" had felt far more like a death threat than this cliff's edge. But when one was born poor, one did what one could to survive. In her case, her arranged marriage to James lent more than survival— it allowed her parents and her three younger siblings to thrive back home in the upper New York countryside. She was a slave to her circumstances. But most women were. It was the nature of things— as natural as the mighty ocean beneath and the ragged rocks at her feet.

"Marilyn. What on earth has gotten into you?"

When Marilyn had first met James— only one week before their marriage, she'd thought his harsh tone covered an insecure interior. She still thought this, yet now, she felt no pity for him. His cruelty didn't allow for it.

Marilyn lifted her chin so that her eyes could meet her husband's. His were cerulean and bright, like a painting she'd once seen of the Mediterranean Sea. This late in the year, the Nantucket Sound was a gray-blue, violent.

"Your hair. It's a mess," James said.

And indeed, it was. She'd stepped out from the Aquinnah Cliffside Overlook Hotel and rushed through the rampant winds to stand here. How could she possibly tell James why she'd needed to stand at the edge? How could she explain that sometimes, she just needed to see the end of the world in order to return to her own?

"I told you. The hotel owner plans to meet with us for dinner."

"Yes, of course."

James' eyes curved toward her stocking feet. The color drained from his cheeks. "Don't tell me you've muddied yourself too much."

Marilyn marched back toward her shoes and slipped them back on. Her stockings had the slightest give of sludge to them since the rain had started across the island of Martha's Vineyard on their car ride from the ferry. She would never tell him and simply live in the slight misery of it. The view had been worth it.

When she'd married James, her mother had suggested that finally, Marilyn would lose sight of her goals and desires. With nearly everything she did, she tried to ensure she didn't. She owed it to herself to cling to some of those just in case.

"Let's meet him then," Marilyn suggested, her voice resolute. "Roger?"

A Vineyard Rebirth

"Robert," James practically growled it. "Robert Sheridan. How many times do I have to tell you?"

In her youth, Marilyn had been known for her memory. She had aced every test and remembered every birthday. It was only since her marriage to James that she'd felt the clouds descend over her mind. She felt drugged, as though a fog enveloped her. She knew this haziness wasn't anything but her own sorrows, however. Sometimes, she opted for a second cocktail after dinner, something she had to hide from James, as he felt that women shouldn't drink as much as men— but it couldn't have been enough to craft such fog day-to-day.

According to her few female friends who gossiped back in New York City, women could only bear men if they'd had a bit to drink. "It's a blessing," a friend had told her once as she'd slipped her a flask. She didn't know how much truth there was to that, though.

The Aquinnah Cliffside Overlook Hotel stood like a force of power and life at the top of the Aquinnah Cliffs, perched on the southwest corner of Martha's Vineyard.

Long ago, in the early 1800s, the hotel had been built as a mansion, right at the end of the island's whaling boom, which had brought along a time of great prosperity, as the island had flourished with tourists and whatever income they wanted to spend on the island. This was Marilyn's first time on Martha's Vineyard, but it was already clear why tourists rushed there from miles around. There was a magic to the air, a rush of life and vitality, even this far into the season. According to James, this was hurricane season— a time of simmering fear of potential destruction. As Marilyn no longer felt she had anything to lose in this life, destruction seemed a beautiful thing. The antithesis of that destruction meant a lifetime with James. It meant delivering his babies. It meant dying by his side.

"Good evening, Mr. Sheridan." James greeted the hotel owner warmly and lifted his hand.

The hotel owner, Robert Sheridan, was six foot three with broad shoulders that looked hard as stone. He was extremely fit. His eyes were a surprising shade of green, and he wore a beard, which matched his thick head of dark hair, a bit longer than what most men wore in the city. It gave him a rugged appeal. Marilyn stopped breathing for a full five seconds.

"Good evening to you, Mr. Peterson," Robert Sheridan returned. "Please, call me Robert."

"Call me James, then. Please, let me introduce my wife, Marilyn."

Marilyn had met countless of James' business associates at this point. But as Robert Sheridan switched his gaze toward her, she felt overcome suddenly, as though his eyes had struck her with a bolt of lightning.

"Marilyn. I trust your journey was a comfortable one?"

Marilyn's voice was lost in her throat. Finally, she whispered, "Yes, and thank you for welcoming us to your beautiful hotel."

Robert leaned back the slightest bit as if taken aback by her pure yet simple words. "I've set aside the presidential suite for the two of you. I trust you'll be comfortable and that you'll let my staff or I know if you require anything. Anything at all."

"My parents informed me that you have the highest quality hotel on all of Martha's Vineyard," James stated. His eyes looked fierce, as though he planned to pounce. He reminded Marilyn of a hunter.

A Vineyard Rebirth

In truth, James had come to this hotel with a single purpose. He was tired of piggybacking off the success of his father. James yearned to make something of himself elsewhere. He wanted to own a number of hotels on Martha's Vineyard, and this, the Aquinnah Cliffside Overlook Hotel, was going to be his first conquest. It didn't matter if Robert Sheridan wanted to sell or not. Once James Peterson had an idea about something, it was difficult to talk him down or convince him otherwise. He was addicted to his fresh ideas, and he did everything in his power to execute them.

"I was out at the edge of the cliff today," Marilyn said suddenly.

James eyed her with suspicion. She was his ticking time bomb.

"Oh? And what did you think of that view?" Robert asked. It seemed unlikely that he would ever drop the intensity of his gaze.

James only looked at her this intensely when he felt she'd eaten too quickly. "You're eating like a pig," he'd told her once with disdain. Since then, she'd hardly touched her meals in front of him and detested that it pleased him.

"It's breathtaking but fierce and wild at the same time," Marilyn whispered then. "The view, I mean. The ocean seems entirely unforgiving— the dark water crashing into the rocks like that. I can't imagine how whalers ever took to the seas like they did, especially when the weather gets bad."

"And they were gone for sometimes five years at a time," Robert returned. "Something difficult to fathom."

"I wonder what they thought of the island after being

away for so long?" Marilyn asked, surprising herself. She was entirely intrigued.

"Robert. We don't mean to take up any more of your time than necessary." James eased into the conversation without pause. "Shall we head to the dining room?"

"Beautiful idea," Robert replied. "I'm famished. With all the responsibilities of this place, I sometimes find it difficult to eat."

They were seated at the table with the best view of the cliff's edge. Again, Marilyn's stomach ached with the glorious intrigue of what it would mean to rush out into the air above the waves and fall to the depths below. What would James say? It pleased her to know that perhaps he wouldn't know what to say. For the first time in his wretched life, perhaps he would be speechless.

James and Robert fell into an easy rhythm of conversation. Marilyn was curious why Robert wasn't married. He looked to be in his late twenties and was certainly handsome, sure of himself, with a beautiful and prominent hotel in his possession (that is if James didn't tear it from him). Robert ordered the best items on the menu— trout, salmon, lobster, mashed potatoes with gravy, roasted Brussels sprouts, and freshly-baked biscuits. Marilyn's mouth salivated at each mention. Robert seemed to catch her excitement. He winked at her and said, "You think that's something? The dessert menu will blow your socks off."

Marilyn blushed as James cast her a menacing look that made her look down at her plate. It was up to her, she knew, to uphold her figure. Dessert wasn't in her daily allowance. Still, it would be rude not to indulge, wouldn't it?

"The tourist season is nearly finished, then?" James

asked. He folded and unfolded his hands beneath the table. Marilyn was perhaps the only person in the world who could sense when James was nervous.

"That's right," Robert returned. "But our hotel stays in operation until November. A number of guests still appreciate the views, our chef, and our surroundings long after the chill dominates the air."

"Marvelous. It means your revenue must be spectacular, as you don't have many inoperable months," James affirmed.

Robert arched his left eyebrow the slightest bit. Marilyn sensed his annoyance and also knew instinctively that James couldn't catch it.

"Perhaps," Robert returned.

Their meal arrived moments later. A beautiful display of pink salmon was set before Marilyn. It glistened beautifully beneath the lamplight. Marilyn lifted her knife and fork swiftly and stabbed them into the pink meat. James gawked at her as Robert grinned widely.

"Darling, please. You don't want to choke," James said through gritted teeth.

"I can handle myself, darling," Marilyn returned flippantly.

"Please. Let Mrs. Peterson eat as much as she pleases," Robert said. His laugh was so familiar to her somehow, as though she'd heard it on a recording long ago. "It's a rare thing to see a woman appreciate her food. So often, the women in this very restaurant look at their plates as though the meat itself might jump up and bite them, instead."

Marilyn's laugh filled the room. It was genuine and it made Robert smile. She dabbed her napkin over her lips and tossed her head back. Again, James glowered at her.

But in front of Robert, she hoped that perhaps he would keep his cruelty at bay.

It was only later, in the presidential suite, that he expressed how upset he was with her behavior.

"You made a fool of yourself at dinner. You can't imagine what this might have done for Robert's analysis of me. If I'm ever to convince him to sell his hotel to me, I must be perceived as a particular kind of man— the kind of man who can keep his wife controlled. What you did tonight was unforgivable. If you continue with this behavior, there will be consequences. Do you understand me?"

James had only hit her once. This was a marked difference from stats whispered from her friends. Many of them were hit weekly. Still, that single slap to the ear-cheek region remained a memory she didn't wish to repeat.

"I said — Marilyn — do you understand me?"

Marilyn flared her nostrils and lifted her chin. The first time they'd made love on their wedding night, she'd bled all over the sheets, and he had called her disgusting.

"I understand you. I always understand you," Marilyn breathed.

"Then, act like it."

Chapter Two

Present Day

"Do you understand me?"

The words echoed through the phone. Kelli had it placed against her ear as she shook with rage at the sound of her soon-to-be ex-husband's voice. Mike had continually made her feel less-than, small, nearly idiotic. It had taken the final nudge from her dear brother, Andrew, before she'd finally had the courage to end the abusive marriage. Since then, Mike had left the island for good and now resided in Rhode Island permanently. Somehow, it wasn't far enough, though. Even his children, the ones they'd created together, didn't miss him. Good riddance was everyone's sentiment. It was just that now, Kelli was left with the legalities of it all. Mike had finally signed the documents required to ensure that the real estate company her parents had passed down to both of them was left only with her name on it.

"Of course I understand you," she blurted back. "Do you understand that I need you to email those documents before the end of the day? I want Susan to file them this afternoon."

Mike grumbled. He had never been a fan of the Sheridan family. Susan, Christine, and Lola had all left the island after high school and made names for themselves off the island. They'd returned a little over a year ago— a sort of storm of emotion and memory in the form of these three beautiful forty-something-year-old women. Mike had done nothing but balk. "They left. They should have stayed in the damn city," he'd insisted over and over until he, himself, had gone.

"I'm pulling up to her law office as we speak, Mike," Kelli hissed into the phone. "Just press send and this can all be over with."

Mike had gone on and on about his contribution to the real estate company and how much he felt he was owed in the wake of his departure. With that said, Kelli felt that she and Susan had come up with a generous offer to buy him out. If he wanted to complain about it and belittle her in the process, then that was his business. The sooner she signed her name on the dotted line and made this all official, the better. Hopefully, she would never speak to him again.

That is, until their children got married— if they invited him at all. That was an iffy one. At the moment, they detested him more than she did.

Susan greeted Kelli in the foyer of the Law Office of Sheridan and Sheridan, a downtown Oak Bluffs spot she and her daughter, Amanda, had opened up the previous winter. Amanda's laughter swirled out from the inner office. Just afterward, there was the booming voice of Sam, who Susan had hired as a sort of manager of the Sunrise Cove. In the wake of that, he and Amanda had struck out for a sort of romance, although, according to Susan, they still wanted to keep everything hush-hush, as Amanda had only just been left at the altar by her long-term boyfriend, Chris. That had certainly been the talk of the island at the time. Of course, the Sheridan women had always been a source of gossip— even in ways the Montgomery family never had been.

"Mike just sent the paperwork, thank goodness," Susan informed her. She wrapped her arms around Kelli and held her close. "I know this has been very traumatic for you."

Kelli grimaced. "But you understand it, right?"

Susan stepped back and nodded exactly once. "My ex-husband and I built our law company together from the ground up. When he bought me out, I thought I might fall apart."

"I guess it's different in this case. I get to keep my parents' business. But you had to move forward and build your own," Kelli admitted.

Kelli stepped into Susan's office and sat at the now-familiar chair across from Susan. Susan placed the stack of papers in front of her and clicked open a blue pen. "You ready for the rest of your life, Kell?"

Kelli wagged her eyebrows playfully. "I was born ready."

It was a funny thing, now that Kelli signed her maiden name: Kelli Montgomery.

"It makes me think of myself as a teenager," she

confessed to Susan after she'd signed. "Like all those years with Mike didn't actually happen."

"I know. But when I dropped Harris as my last name, I felt a sense of freedom, like a weight had been lifted from my shoulders," Susan said thoughtfully.

"Did it make you sad not to have the same last name as your children?" Kelli asked.

"Maybe at the beginning, but they never brought it up. And I found myself slipping back into the Sheridan name like an old skin. Now, I suppose, I'm Susan Sheridan Frampton— but we haven't officially changed it over."

Kelli's smile brightened. "How are things going with Scott? And the house?"

"You know Scott. He loves a good project," Susan admitted with a laugh. "The place is about as beautiful as can be. We agree on almost everything, even down to what wallpaper to put in the bathroom. It's almost disgusting. It makes me laugh to think of all the stupid fights I had with my ex, Richard, throughout our marriage. We fought for days about what kind of countertops to put in our kitchen. Can you imagine Scott putting up any kind of fuss like that?"

"Scott loves you to bits. If you wanted to live in the woods without a kitchen altogether, he'd go for it," Kelli said. She then paused before adding, "You got so lucky, Susan. After your divorce, you and Scott found one another again. I thought Mike was my forever. And now, I don't know what to do except get over the trauma he caused me. All that pain. What was it for?"

"I don't think it's up to us to understand why people hurt us the way they do," Susan breathed. "I just think we do have a responsibility to uphold our feelings and our emotions and try to heal the best we can. When Richard and I split up, I told myself to *take it one day at a time*. And that one day at a time approach has got me to where I am today. Perhaps that's stupid to say. But it's the truth."

* * *

"Can you still meet me at Mom and Dad's?" This was Kelli's little sister, Claire, who had just called her when she returned to her vehicle after signing all the documentation.

Kelli ran a hand through her long hair. Oak Bluffs traffic was vibrant. Tourists seemed overly willing to walk out in front of cars and end it all in search of the best ice cream cone or top-rated seafood dinner. Kelli knew better than to mock the tourists continually; after all, they were Martha's Vineyard's bread and butter and had been since after the whaling boom. All islanders knew that.

"I don't know, Claire. I'm so zonked. Mike called me four times today to go over the paperwork before he officially signed. The first call came around five-thirty in the morning."

"He'll never change, will he? Well, at least you're rid of him now for good."

"Hopefully. I can't help but freak out that I'll find him back at the house, waiting for me like Michael from the *Halloween* movies."

Claire's laughter was like music. Kelli's heart lightened just the slightest bit. Finally, she found an opening in traffic and eased her vehicle from the side of the road. Her home beckoned— but still, Claire rode her hard to stop by her parents'.

"It'll take like four seconds," Claire insisted. "I just

want your advice about this floral arrangement for a wedding this weekend. You have a really artistic eye, Kell." Claire owned her own successful flower shop in Oak Bluffs. Normally, she didn't ask for assistance. Still, Kelli was too exhausted to overthink her request.

"Said no one ever," she replied instead.

"Kelli! I swear. If you stop by, I'll never ask you for anything else. Ever."

Kelli was a sucker for her younger siblings and always had been. Charlotte, Claire, and Andrew— especially Andrew, were her world. Steven, her older brother, had always been able to take care of himself. Kelli was endlessly grateful, even now, that Andy had returned to the Vineyard the previous Christmas. He had stayed away far too long. With each passing decade, Kelli had felt the very fabric of her family disintegrate. With him back now, they could stitch themselves back together again— better and stronger than ever before.

At a red light, Kelli texted her daughter, Lexi, about her whereabouts.

> KELLI: I have to run to Grandma and Grandpa's house. Claire needs some help. Maybe we could order pizza tonight? If you don't have plans. XOXO.

Normally, Lexi texted back in three seconds flat. She was eighteen and glued to her phone. But as Kelli pressed lightly on the gas and drove the few more miles toward the house where she had grown up, no messages came through. Lexi knew what kind of day this had been for her; she knew the harrowing feeling in Kelli's stomach. At least, she'd thought she had translated this to her daughter. Lexi herself had tried and failed to get her mother to eat dinner the previous few nights. The anxiety had been overwhelming, almost destructive.

Claire was waiting for her on the front porch of her parents' house. She wore a bright smile and lifted an enormous bouquet into the air as Kelli stepped through the lush grass to greet her. Kelli tried a smile but struggled to lift it.

"There she is. My beautiful big sis."

It was a humid day, and the drive from the law office had been sticky and warm. Moisture billowed up on Kelli's forehead and beneath her arms.

"I don't feel particularly beautiful," Kelli offered with a laugh. "Is this the bouquet you wanted me to check out?"

Claire wagged her eyebrows playfully. She placed the bouquet to the side, removed a little packet of tissues, and began to dot one across Kelli's forehead. Kelli bucked back and cried, "What are you doing?"

"Just hold still for a second. And maybe... hmm..." Claire leafed into her purse and drew out a tube of lipstick.

"What's gotten into you?" Kelli demanded. She suddenly felt like her teenage self, annoyed with her younger sister's antics.

"Just put this on. Trust me."

Kelli rolled her eyes. "I don't care what I look like in front of Mom and Dad anymore."

Claire pressed the tube of lipstick against Kelli's chest and locked eyes with her. "Just trust me on this one, okay?"

An idea shivered in the back of Kelli's mind. She glanced toward the front door, then at the flowers. The driveway was empty, save for Claire's and her parents' vehicles. Still, that didn't mean others hadn't parked elsewhere.

"You didn't," Kelli breathed.

Claire furrowed her brow. Kelli heaved a sigh, gripped the lipstick, and tapped it delicately across her lower and upper lips, then rubbed them together.

"You know I hate surprises," Kelli whispered.

"Nobody hates surprises," Claire insisted, flashing her sister the biggest smile.

"I do."

When Kelli pressed open the front door, everyone she had ever loved leaped up from behind the couch, the hall closet, and the back kitchen. Her father and mother, her sister, Charlotte, her brothers, Andrew and Steven, along with Steven's wife, Laura, and Andrew's newer girlfriend, Beth. Beth's little son, Will, who was on the spectrum, leaped up from behind the couch and flung glitter through the air. The Sheridan sisters were there, including Susan, who'd obviously raced from the law office to arrive before Kelli. All Montgomery and Sheridan family members were accounted for, in fact— and all of them hollered out at once.

"CONGRATULATIONS, KELLI!"

A banner echoed this sentiment overhead. It looked like maybe Will had painted the thing, as the words were slightly crooked. This made Kelli love it all the more.

Christine Sheridan and her niece, Audrey, appeared from the kitchen next. Christine's pregnant belly bulged beneath a beautiful cake, something she'd baked and decorated herself. It was heavy with ornate flowers and thick frosting, along with the words -- OUR FAVORITE REAL ESTATE WOMAN. Kelli laughed and swiped away a tear.

"The business is all yours now." Her father beamed as he stepped forward and placed a kiss on her cheek. "We couldn't be more proud that you've taken over our baby for yourself. Your mother and I built that real estate company together over many decades of love and hard labor. It was our dream that one of our children would take the reins and make it their own."

"And now, that horrible man is gone," her mother added brightly. "And the business is back to being only a labor of love."

Kelli beamed, even as she felt a stab of fear and regret. There had been eras of the previous ten years when she'd felt that she and Mike had operated as well or even better, in some respects, than her parents had. Mike had been aggressive in sales in ways she'd never been capable of, probably because he was a bully, through and through. Kelli worried she wouldn't be able to sell as much as he had. She worried their revenue would falter.

But those were worries she couldn't verbalize now. Not at the party that her family had thrown her in full support of her next era as a sole business owner. She shivered at the thought.

Kelli felt like a ghost at her own funeral. It was a difficult thing to walk through the party guests, hugging her family members and her children. She could still feel the volatile words from Mike echoing through her ears. According to her therapist, the trauma she had gone through wouldn't just fall off of her. It was something she had to attack head-on. It was something she had to carry.

"There she is— the guest of honor." Andy took two strides closer and wrapped her in a bear hug, placing his chin gently on her shoulder.

She shook the slightest bit, proof of her true feelings. Andy leaned back and furrowed his brow.

"You're not so thrilled with this surprise party, are you?"

Kelli's nostrils flared. "You see right through me, don't you?"

"It's a bad habit. We're linked."

"I guess." Kelli swallowed hard and glanced out at the sea of people across the porch and yard, which led up to a sandy beach that lined the Vineyard Sound. "I love all of these people with everything in my soul, but right now, I kind of want to curl up into a ball and hide."

Andrew laughed. "It's difficult to hide from the Montgomery-Sheridan clan. They're always looking for a reason to party, and they don't like to let you wallow. I tried to wallow for the rest of my life and now look at me — back on the Vineyard for eight months now, with no sign of leaving. I hadn't been to a party in years."

"And now, you're cursed with regular family barbecues."

Andy chuckled. "I know it's tough when you're feeling low. If you want, I can make an excuse for you. Help you slip out the back."

Lexi appeared alongside Kelli and Andy with a mischievous grin. She held a plate of cake, a slice that seemed slathered with extra frosting. Kelli gripped the edge of Lexi's fork and took a small bite from the edge as Lexi protested playfully.

"Get your own piece!"

Kelli's heart brightened. "But yours looked so tasty!"

Will scampered up then and tugged at Lexi's arm. "Lexi, remember when you said you wanted to learn more about dinosaurs? I have some things you might be interested in."

Lexi's eyes widened in surprise. "Right." She nodded toward Andy and Kelli. "Seems like I have some studying to do."

Lexi and Will moved toward the edge of the porch, where Will had set up a number of his dinosaur toys. Kelli chuckled as Andy swept his fingers through his hair.

"That kid is really something," Kelli commented.

"He's a handful," Andy added. "But the best kind."

"And Beth? How's she been?"

Beth was in conversation with Lola near the waterline. It was a rare thing as of late to see Beth at a family function, as her hours at the hospital had ramped up over the summer.

Andy's eyes glistened. "How do I say this? She changed my life. I'm not sure where I would be without her."

Kelli felt on the verge of tears but managed to hold them back. She was so happy for her brother. She wrapped a hand around Andy's wrist and squeezed gently. "I hope you tell her that as much as you can."

"I do. She's getting annoyed at it," Andy said with a laugh. "But don't worry. She knows how much I love her."

"Wow. Love." Kelli felt punched in the stomach. Romantic love had long ago seemed like a thing other people were allowed, and not her. Especially as Mike's love had turned increasingly cruel and sinister, she had told herself over and over again that Mike simply loved "differently." He loved with aggression which, in her mind for a while, was more passionate, more charged.

But it hadn't been right. It had never been right.

"Maybe I'll grab my own slice of cake," Kelli said.

"I'll come with you."

The brother-sister duo headed into the kitchen, where Steven and his eldest son, Jonathon, were in conversation with Amanda Harris, who discussed more details regarding Susan's recent, very intense court case, which had involved a young woman from the island who'd been accused of murdering her boyfriend. The case had wrapped up in June and resulted in the girl's innocence in the eyes of the court. It had been a blessing for the law office and proven Susan as one of the top attorneys on the east coast, even without her ex-husband. As Amanda discussed the case in more detail, she beamed with pride.

"That's the women in the Montgomery-Sheridan clan to a T," Steven stated as he glanced toward Kelli and nodded firmly, proof that he included her in this, as well. "Between Kelli, Susan, Lola, Claire, Charlotte, and Christine— along with the next generation of women, like you, Amanda, I mean wow. The world doesn't know quite what to make of any of you. You're all a force to be reckoned with."

Kelli's smile faltered. She splayed a slice of cake on her plate and felt suddenly doomed by the approaching weeks. How could she possibly keep up this real estate company on her own? Was she actually strong enough to see this through herself? She was, after all, a Montgomery woman. She felt the most unsure in her life, hollowed out and strange. She knew better than to think that this cake would fill her up. Yet even still, she took a small bite and it was so delicious. Soon afterward, she went to the front porch, which was empty of family members, and wept for all she had lost.

Chapter Three

She had to sell that old place. She had to. It had been her parents' years-long terror, a property that seemed haunted or cursed, as countless potential buyers had come through the island and eventually backed out. The selling of the property would be an iconic one and a blessing for Kelli, considering it would be the biggest sale she would ever close. It would also prove to herself and to her entire family that she could handle the real estate company on her own.

The day's potential buyer was a man named Gregory Bellow. Like many of the previous potential buyers, he'd come in from New York City, and he reeked of money and a lack of understanding of the island and its many locals. Kelli tried her best to see beyond this. After all, he had enough money to take this property off her hands. What did she care what he did with the old place once it was his?

"Wonderful to finally meet you in person, Mr. Bellow," Kelli greeted with a genuine smile. She held out a hand and shook his as firmly as she could. In past years, she'd noted that potential clients had shaken Mike's hand with a firmer grip, showing their respect for him and their lesser respect for her. It was a man's world— and now, she had to play that role. Otherwise, her company could go under.

"And you as well, Ms. Montgomery." Mr. Bellow dropped her handshake and beamed. He looked to be in his sixties with wide-set gray eyes. His cologne was just a hint too powerful, and Kelli's nostrils flared despite her best efforts to keep them in.

"Shall we head over to the property?"

"I would love it. I can't wait to see it in person. The photos you sent activated my imagination, to say the least."

Kelli's laughter sounded almost fake to her own ears. She waved goodbye to her secretary, a woman Mike had hired years before named Brittany. The secretary had witnessed a number of Mike's insults and had sent Kelli a gift basket after she had finally left Mike. Mike hadn't exactly been kind to Brittany over the years, either. Kelli was surprised that she had stuck around. Kelli walked toward the door and caught Brittany's eye again as she mouthed to Kelli, "Good luck."

"So this place was destroyed back in the fifties?" They were seated in her car as Kelli drove Mr. Bellow westward and south toward the Aquinnah Cliffs.

"1943, actually."

He turned to her and said, "A hurricane, huh?"

"Yes. It doesn't happen often that a hurricane rips through the Vineyard, but when they come, they come without mercy," she told him.

"Quite romantic to think of this old place," Mr.

Bellow continued. "It was built in the early 1800s, correct?"

"Yes. It's broken my heart over the years to think of what the old place might look like had it not been destroyed."

Mr. Bellow was quiet until they reached the old cliffside resort. Out front, an ancient sign still remained, slightly crooked, looking like a relic from a previous era. It read: AQUINNAH CLIFFSIDE OVERLOOK HOTEL in an old-world font. As she often did when she approached the old property, Kelli held her breath for a long time. It seemed remarkable that the place had ever thrived with its glorious tourists and long stretches of bright, summertime activities. It seemed remarkable that it had ever been anything but a dilapidated haunted mansion.

Kelli parked the car and stepped out, announcing their arrival. "This is it— the old hotel."

Mr. Bellow stood at the edge of the property and blinked up at the old historic building. "Wow. The hurricane took out more than you could really see in photographs," he said with the slightest hint of disappointment.

It might have been a little true that the photos Kelli had sent had been taken at particular, artful angles— ones that had eliminated much of the damage. She and Brittany had discussed this tactic at length, deciding that ultimately, once buyers arrived at the property, they would see what a remarkable place it truly was in person.

As she and Mr. Bellow walked up toward the mansion, with its remarkable wrap-around porch and its entire leftward area that had fallen through to the base of the mansion below, she watched as Mr. Bellow's face took on a similar stance as previous potential buyers. He was clearly disappointed and worse, his expression stated she had wasted his time. Even as she explained that the area that had sunken in was where the old ballroom and restaurant had been, he looked on toward the cliffside doubtfully.

"Would you like to walk to the edge? It's really a beautiful view."

Mr. Bellow cleared his throat. "I've seen the ocean already. Thank you, Ms. Montgomery."

Mike had wanted to tell potential buyers that it was possible to clear out the old mansion and start over with the property. Kelli couldn't bring herself to say such a thing. She felt attached to the place, even in its ragged state. It was a portion of Martha's Vineyard history. It seemed to scream with memories, waiting to be uncovered.

But Mr. Bellow didn't hear their cries.

And in fact, the next three potential buyers over the next week didn't hear the cries, either. Kelli was exasperated. She sat at her desk in the real estate office, the very one her father had sat at for a number of decades before he and her mother had passed the company on to her. She curved her hands over her cheeks and let out a low sigh. Brittany made her way to the doorway, placed her hands on her hips, and said, "Have you eaten the lunch I brought you? You didn't, did you?"

Kelli's lips tugged into a smile. "You know me too well."

Brittany clacked her heels over to the refrigerator and pulled out the salad that she had purchased from the organic store down the street. She placed it again on Kelli's desk along with a fork.

"It's why I'm here, you know."

"To guilt me into eating healthier?"

"To take care of you," Brittany corrected her, tapping a nail on top of the plastic container. "Office stuff, life stuff— all of it."

Kelli blew the air out of her lungs. "I'm not sure what I would do without you."

"I know what you would do. Starve yourself and then eat French fries to make up for it, and I just can't let that happen. I won't hear of it!"

Kelli let out a little laugh as she unsnapped the top from the salad and peered at the wide selection of spinach greens, bright red onions and shining green peppers. "Mm, nutrients."

"Don't joke about nutrition. It keeps us all sane." Brittany furrowed her brow. "I guess it didn't go well this morning with that potential buyer?"

"Everyone just looks at the old mansion and scoffs at the amount of work it would take to build it back up, I think," Kelli admitted. She pieced through the salad delicately and stabbed a black olive with her fork tongs. It was a jolt of salty goodness on her tongue. Her brain suddenly came into operation again.

"When I see that place, I see all this romantic potential," Brittany said. "If I had the money and the time, I'd love to fix it up. Oh, but you know how obsessed me and my husband are with all those fixer-upper TV shows. They're so soothing to watch."

Kelli chuckled. "Wish I could sell it to you. That old place could use your ideas and your commitment to the old, romantic ways of the island."

"An islander, through and through, just like you." Brittany grinned, tapping herself on the upper chest proudly. Her smile faltered slightly. "But Sanderson Real Estate has offered again to take the property off your hands."

Kelli gripped the fork harder till her knuckles turned white. "The nerve they have to keep asking."

"I know. I know. I just figured I'd tell you, just in case the idea sounded appealing this time around."

Kelli hesitated with her fork lifted. A leaf of spinach hovered in the air. "It would be such a relief, wouldn't it? Not to have that old place on my conscience?"

"I figured the answer was a no. I'll call them back right away."

"Thank you, Brit."

Brittany closed the door. Kelli dropped her fork again. Her appetite was gone. Why couldn't she sell this property herself? She felt completely void of purpose. She'd read countless self-help articles online about divorced women who "found themselves" during the year post-break-up. Why couldn't she be one of those women? Why was she floundering?

Several hours later, Kelli jumped into her car. She had half-planned to stop at the old boutique she still ran, now with a great deal of help from Lexi. But some invisible force dragged her westward, toward the cliffs. Before she knew it, she was standing on the old Aquinnah Cliffside Overlook Hotel property with her heart in her throat. The last tower on the old mansion still struck out toward the pink and purple sunset sky above, as though it still had hope of supporting people once again. The staircase that led up to the top of the tower had been rotted out long ago. Nobody had dared go up there. In fact, back in the sixties, there had been an accident— some teenager trying

A Vineyard Rebirth

his hand at being a daredevil and winding up with a broken leg.

It's funny to think that the sixties had been only twenty years after the hurricane. Now, the old hurricane had been nearly seventy years ago.

"I wish I could build you up myself," she whispered to the property as her heart surged. And even now, she could close her eyes and imagine the streams of new tourists as they rushed around the old property. Perhaps there would be a tennis court, a croquet area, and a gorgeous bright blue swimming pool. Perhaps they would have horses to borrow and gorgeous stables to house them in. Perhaps they would build the ballroom back up to its previous status and hold classical balls, ones that would require men and women to wear outfits reminiscent of the twenties and thirties of the previous century.

There was so much to imagine about this place. Why couldn't her clients see that?

Kelli walked along the cliff's edge, her eyes trained on the horizon. Sailboats dotted the edges of what seemed to be the earth with their sails lifted with the wind. Kelli hadn't been on a sailboat the entire summer. Perhaps that's why she felt so despondent? She knew deep down there were a number of other reasons.

Kelli reached the edge of a trail and peered down at the beach below. There, a couple stood as the water rushed forth, frothing over the rocks. They were picture-perfect with their hands latched together. Kelli and Mike hadn't done anything like that in years. She had hardly looked him in the eye in ten years. The last time they'd been romantic with one another, she had felt so broken and used. There had been no love at all.

Suddenly, the man down below dropped to his knee.

He gripped the woman's hand delicately as he performed this very private, very beautiful act— a proposal. Instinctively, Kelli stepped back, wanting to give them their time alone. But then, a jolt of recognition came over her.

It was Andy. Her baby brother. Her baby brother was now proposing to Beth, the woman who had helped him rediscover life all over again.

Tears filled Kelli's eyes as a sob escaped her lips, and she covered it with her hand. This was remarkable.

Down below, Beth nodded and threw her arms around Andy. They stayed in the warmth of that embrace for a long time. Even a year ago, Kelli hadn't thought she would ever see Andy again. Now, here he was, making a commitment to the love of his life. It was a beautiful thing.

Kelli resented the fact that it made her feel even more alone. Her marriage had ended, and now her baby brother was just starting. It was so funny how these things worked. She tried to shove this thought aside, but there it was, a little stone of jealousy in her stomach. It didn't negate her happiness for Andy; it simply reminded her of her own sorrows. She couldn't help it, especially with everything so fresh.

She knew Andy had brought Beth there for the privacy. Kelli refused to ruin that moment for them. She rushed back for her car and drove toward the main road, her eyesight blurry with tears. The radio DJ played an old Simon and Garfunkel song about loneliness. Kelli's heart screamed every word.

Chapter Four

It was the weekend of the Fourth of July. Almost on cue, as though to add to the curse of her reality, the air conditioner cut out mid-way through the morning on one of the hotter days of the year. The repair guy couldn't make it till Tuesday, which left Lexi and Kelli in tank tops and shorts, sweating profusely on the couch as they stared with glazed eyes at the television. They'd decided to close the boutique that day, as nobody was really in the mood to shop with this extreme heat wave.

"Grandma says we should come over." Lexi glanced at her phone and then tossed it on the couch next to her. She took a large swig of ice water, her eyes only half-open. "She says we're crazy to stay here."

"Okay. Can you carry me to the bathroom to take a shower? I don't think I can move a muscle," Kelli returned, side-glancing her daughter.

Lexi chuckled. "I was going to ask you the same thing."

"We're pathetic." Kelli gripped the remote control

and turned the screen black. In a moment, she had forgotten whatever it was they had been watching. Lexi didn't protest because she had already forgotten, too.

Finally, Lexi stood and stretched her arms toward the ceiling, making them crack. "Grandma says we should go through the old stuff in the attic before everyone else arrives."

"I've been asking her for those clothes to put in the boutique for years." Kelli stood, also stretching. "Wonder why she changed her mind now."

"That attic has always been a mystery to me," Lexi affirmed. "Let's just hope there's not too much polyester up there. Guessing that won't sell too well at the boutique."

"Oh, you should have seen what your grandmother wore in the eighties: big, puffy sleeves and enormous glasses. And I caught her smoking sometimes. Just what everyone did back then, I guess."

Lexi wrinkled her nose. "Ew."

"Glad you think that way, honey. Times changed for the better."

"Yeah. Now, we spend all our time with our phones instead of socializing over cigarettes," Lexi said with a cheeky grin. "The future is a beautiful thing."

Kelli and Lexi both took chilly showers and headed off to Kelli's childhood home, where they had planned a combined Fourth of July and engagement party to celebrate Andrew and Beth. Needless to say, Kelli's mother, Kerry, was head-over-heels for the news from her prodigal son. Her cheeks had taken on a bright color, and she climbed up the attic ladder like a schoolgirl as she talked about the menu she'd prepared for the later party.

"I do hope Beth isn't overwhelmed. She can sometimes be so quiet while our family can be so..."

"Overwhelming?" Lexi tried as she scampered up the ladder after her.

"I was going to say exuberant," Kerry said.

Kelli hadn't been in her parents' attic in decades. She half-remembered playing up there, in the dust and haze of a long-ago afternoon, probably with Steven, as he was the closest to her in age. The attic was lined with boxes and old trunks; piles of books lay near the far wall, and boxes labeled TOYS were aligned near the tiny window. A small lightbulb hung from the slanted ceiling. Kerry gripped it and clanked the little string, which resulted in, to Kelli's surprise, light.

"How old is that lightbulb?" she asked her mother.

"Good question. Guess it'll hold out a little longer," Kerry returned.

The first trunk was filled with a number of mid-grade clothing items from the seventies and eighties. Lexi's face was difficult to read as she pieced through the items and created NO, YES, and MAYBE piles. Kelli guessed that she made the YES pile much bigger than she might have, had her grandmother not been beside her.

"Oh, that old thing," Kerry said, regarding a particularly trashy-looking dark purple dress. "I wore that when your father took me dancing in the city. Goodness, it feels like a lifetime ago." She beamed and lifted the dress to align across her figure.

"Looks like it still fits," Lexi pointed out.

"Sure does. Not sure it fits the style or my age," Kerry replied sadly. "Do you think anyone would want it?"

Lexi pondered this for a moment. "Don't you want to hold onto it? Maybe as a keepsake?"

Kerry nodded quickly and clung to it harder. "Yeah, don't take it. Not this dress." Her eyes flashed with a sudden thought. "And if I'm not mistaken, that night of dancing in the city resulted in a baby—"

"Grandma!"

Kelli loved the sudden mischievous nature of her mother's face. It was a rare thing to get a story like this out of her mother. She had always stood for womanly propriety. One didn't say such things— not even around family.

But now, Kerry shrugged and gazed longingly at the dress. "It must have been Steven or maybe Kelli. Maybe we got a sitter for the weekend, or Steven stayed with Wes. It's difficult to say now that it's been so long. But I can still remember your father's face when he took me to that club. He looked so handsome."

When they reached the bottom of that chest, they moved on to the next: more clothes, more jewelry, and more stories. Kerry poured them over Lexi and Kelli as though she'd been dying to give her things away and to tell the inner aching of her soul for decades. Despite Kelli's recent sorrows, she still felt the magic behind her mother's words and longed to lap up everything and cling to these elements of her mother that Kerry had long ago hidden.

"You were something of a wild card, I guess, Grandma," Lexi commented with a slight grin.

"I guess so. Your grandfather used to say he couldn't believe I ever settled down," Kerry said mischievously. "Of course, back then, that's what you did. But I don't want you to rush yourself, Lexi girl. Go out there and live as well as you can."

"Did you hear that, Mom? I think Grandma's telling me to go out and take risks," Lexi said.

"Don't give her the wrong idea, Mom," Kelli joked. "She'll go off and steal a yacht or something."

"And if she gives me a ride in that yacht? I'm all for it." Kerry shook with laughter as she opened another trunk near the far wall. "Oh, my goodness. No clothes in here."

Kerry leaned forward the slightest bit to take stock of the trunk. Within were what seemed to be yesterday's important files. Kelli lifted the first folder and said, "Ah, look. It's the deed to this very house. I wondered where that was. We paid it all off so many years ago that, well— stuff like that doesn't matter so much to us these days. I suppose it will happen sometime when we— well." She gave a light shrug.

Kelli wasn't sure how to talk about any of that— the approaching years. She supposed the dialogue would come to her when it was necessary. As it stood, Kerry still seemed so young and vibrant to her. Perhaps she didn't feel that way on the inside. Kelli had never asked her mother what it felt to be in her seventies. The question seemed somehow rude, as though it drew attention to the passing of time, which normally you were supposed to ignore.

But it still had its way with you, regardless.

Lexi grabbed the clothing items for the boutique and headed for the ladder. "I'll run these out to the car."

"Thanks, hon." Kelli kneeled in front of this newly opened trunk and followed her mother's eyes over the yellowing pages. "What's all this other stuff?" She was scared to touch them, scared they might disintegrate between her fingers.

"Looks like old letters." Kerry sifted through some and gently unfolded various pages. Her lips formed a circle as her eyes scanned the documents. "Wow. This one is from my Grandma Sheridan to her future husband, my grandfather. They're the ones who built the Sunrise Cove."

Kelli had heard the story, of course— but she had never met her great-grandparents on the Sheridan side, as they had died terribly young. Heck, she'd never even met her grandparents.

"I hate that we're apart, darling, but I know when I return to the Vineyard, our lives will be cast out before us like the glittering stars above," Kerry read from the letter as her own eyes twinkled with tears. "Goodness. People don't write like that anymore, do they?"

"They certainly don't. It makes our text message correspondences look weak, huh?"

"At least we don't have to wait for weeks to receive them," Kerry said as she folded the letter once more. "Goodness. I can just picture her writing that. And that penmanship is divine. Mine is a scrawl in comparison."

"And even yours would win penmanship awards, Mom."

They continued through the chest, gently removing each item and organizing the pieces in the space in front of their knees. Kelli's own had begun to ache; she couldn't even imagine what her mother's felt like. Still, neither of them found space to complain.

"Goodness. What is this?" Her mother lifted a larger, rolled-up piece of old paper— so old that it was crackled and water stained. It had an aura to it; it spoke of a time before the twentieth century. Kelli felt lost for words.

She peeked within the rolled-up paper and noted various designs within, sharp lines that reminded her of old architectural drawings she'd seen at a museum. Her heart raced.

"These are old blueprints, I think."

"Wow," Kerry breathed. "I wonder why I've never seen them before. Should we open them?"

"I don't know. I'm scared that they're too damaged for us to handle properly. Maybe I could take them to an antiquarian."

Kerry nodded stoically. "That would be fascinating, wouldn't it?"

She returned to the chest and leafed through a number of newspaper clippings after that. Many regarded both Wesley and Kerry's childhood. Kerry had been born in 1949, Wes in 1953. In one newspaper photograph, both Wes and Kerry stood with other children in front of the schoolhouse in Oak Bluffs, where they'd all gone together until age twelve.

"Goodness. Look at this dress!" Kerry laughed at the little lace get-up the child Kerry wore in the photograph. "I look terribly uncomfortable. I guess I'm eight here? Little Wes is only four. I think our parents pushed him to go to school so they could work more at the Sunrise Cove without having him get underfoot. He would kill me if he heard me say that now. After all, that inn is his life, his love— it's his everything. But before that, it was our parents' to love. Before they, too, died so young."

Her eyes grew shadowed at that very thought.

Other newspaper clippings seemed even older. Wonderfully, two or three of them reported the hurricane of 1943, along with a longer article about the destruction of the Aquinnah Cliffside Overlook Hotel. Kelli made a mental note to read more about that later.

Slowly, one of Kerry's hands crept over what looked

like a diary in the far corner of the chest. The skin on her hand was terribly thin, like paper.

"This must be my mother's diary," Kerry breathed. "I remember her writing in them when I was younger, but I just never knew where they ended up. We must have moved this chest into the attic when we were first married. My goodness, how time gets away from us."

Kerry's eyes shone with a mix of fear and sorrow. Kelli sensed they'd driven too far from their day's purpose.

"Maybe we can do the diary read another day," Kelli offered brightly. "The others will probably come by soon."

Her mother looked at her with confused, hollow eyes.

"You know. Andy's engagement party?"

"Yes. Yes, of course." Kerry shook her head to clear the inner cobwebs. "I'll put all this stuff back. We can dive through it later. At least we managed to find a few items for the boutique. Such fun to imagine my clothes living new lives! I certainly won't be wearing them any time soon."

Kelli watched from above as her mother stepped down the attic ladder gently. Kelli placed the blueprints at the top of the ladder, turned to place her feet on the rungs, then followed in her mother's footsteps, careful to grab the blueprints on the way. She had a funny hunch about what the blueprints were for— but she didn't want to hope too desperately. Things didn't always turn out the right way for Kelli. In fact, it seemed like most didn't at all. Why might this time be any different?

Chapter Five

Already, several guests had arrived for the Fourth of July and Engagement Party celebrations. Uncle Wes hovered in the kitchen with a little bowl of chips in his hand while his granddaughter, Audrey, stood several feet away from him with what looked to be an M&M lifted near her own face. Audrey's firstborn, baby Max, slept in a little wrap over her breasts. Still, she spoke in a normal voice as she said, "Are you sure you remember how, Grandpa?"

"What do you mean? As if I'd forget my newfound skill," Uncle Wes replied with a funny, youthful scowl.

"It's just that yesterday, you made me doubt all the hard work we've put into this over the past year," Audrey returned.

Wes lifted his chin. "I told you. I was distracted. You were playing that useless hip hop music."

"You told me you liked Cardi B now, Grandpa!"

"Sure. She's okay. But you had that other one on." Wes's eyes shifted toward Kelli in greeting.

"Has your granddaughter taught you all the music of the twenty-first century?" Kelli asked with a funny smile.

"She's keeping me hip, I guess," Uncle Wes affirmed.

"Watch this, Kell." Audrey's voice sizzled with confidence. She lurched her hand back, then tossed an M&M through the air. On cue, Wes opened his mouth to allow the bite-sized chocolate morsel to land precisely on his tongue. Audrey hollered excitedly and then placed a hand steadily on Max's head.

It was remarkable to Kelli that Audrey, at the tender age of twenty, was a mother. Still, she supposed she'd been a mother around that age as well. Funny to think of her back then. Just a girl, playing pretend. When had she become an adult in her own right? Was she even one, now? Sometimes, she still felt like this was all pretend.

"Impressive," Kelli told Wes as he grinned sheepishly. "You've been working on that all year?"

"Sure have. When Amanda lets us keep exciting snacks in the house, at least," Audrey told her. "She's a stickler for salads."

"Sounds awful." Kelli chuckled as she poured herself a glass of wine, then headed back into the living area, where she caught Beth coming in from the porch. Beth's skin glowed beautifully. She looked youthful and radiant, on the verge of the next phase of her life.

"Beth! There's my future sister-in-law."

Kelli wrapped her arms around Beth and held her close for a moment. She still hadn't confessed that she had witnessed the proposal. Perhaps she never would, so that it could be theirs to have forever.

Beth lifted a hand after they released each other to show off her wedding ring. Andrew had done well; it was a vintage ring with a dark blue stone, something reminiscent of the Art Deco period. Kelli whistled.

"Why does Andy have such a hard time dressing if he can pick out such a nice ring?" Kelli teased just as Andrew stepped into the living room with Will by his side.

"I took a blind guess on that thing," Andrew confessed with a funny smile. "Guess it worked?"

"More than worked, baby brother," Kelli corrected. "I'd say you picked a dream engagement ring."

Andrew pressed his lips against Kelli's cheek. Their father, Trevor, came into the living room with a beer lifted and his eyes bright.

"Here's to the happy couple!" he cried.

"Dad. Not everyone is here yet. We can keep the speeches and toasts for later," Andy teased.

"On the contrary, I just don't think we can have enough toasts," Trevor affirmed. "Where's my darling bride?"

Kerry hovered in the kitchen now, preparing the platter of pre-formed burgers, which one of the men would soon take to the grill.

"In here, honey! Slaving away in the kitchen, like always!"

"Is she complaining again?" Trevor teased after cracking a wide smile. He stepped through and kissed Kerry on the cheek, matching Andy.

Again, Kelli's heart lifted at this show of affection between her parents. She marveled that she'd made such a mistake in marrying Mike. Where had she gone wrong? Was she undeserving of love?

Will latched onto her elbow and tugged it. She glanced down and met his stern gaze.

"What's up, Will?"

"You look sad," he told her. Always, he pointed out factual information.

"Will..." Beth warned.

"It's all right, Beth." Kelli kneeled the slightest bit so that she could match Will's gaze. "I'm not that sad. I'm just thinking about something in my life. And all the things I'm grateful for, too. Are you grateful for anything?"

Will considered this. He then pointed toward Andy as he blurted, "I'm grateful for him. He makes my mom smile."

"You can't really ask for anything better than that, can you, Will?"

Will shook his head as Beth's eyes filled with tears. Kelli thought that probably, all these years, Beth thought she would live forever as a single mom. How strange that everything could shift so quickly. Almost on cue, the clouds could break in the sky, and you could find yourself with nothing but blue above.

"A friend is headed over here," Uncle Wes said to Trevor as he stuck another M&M in his mouth. "An old friend who left the island years ago."

"Oh? Do I remember him?" Trevor asked.

"Not sure." Wes furrowed his brows for a moment. It was a familiar expression these days, as he'd been diagnosed with early-onset dementia more than a year before. Still, with help from his daughters and granddaughters, he fought tooth and nail to cling to the memories he still had and even made more, day after day. It was remarkable.

Even still, Kelli knew the story would end badly. The only question was when.

A Vineyard Rebirth

"His name is Van Tress," Wes finally affirmed. "Mark Van Tress. He's a little older than both of us. Mid-seventies by now, I believe. He's on vacation. I told him about our little get-together and said my sister always has enough food to share."

"Oh, brother," Kerry hollered from the kitchen. "Here we go again."

"I think I remember him," Trevor said. "He hung around the Sunrise Cove for a while, didn't he?"

"Always demanded to buy it," Wes chuckled. "But I never let him. I told him it ran in the family, and it wouldn't go to anyone but my daughters one day." He paused and then glanced out toward the back porch, where Susan and Christine stood in rapt conversation. "I guess that process has already begun."

Mark Van Tress arrived several minutes later. He was a spry older gentleman, clearly from a good deal of money, and he greeted everyone warmly, many with gentle kisses on the cheek, as though he'd gone to Europe too many times and now needed everyone to know about it. Still, despite his clear money background, he was joyous and colorful, remembering everyone's names almost immediately and sending winks across the room to those he couldn't meet quite yet.

"There are so many people here. Trevor and Wes, your families have really grown. And look at that little bitty baby! Wes, don't tell me you're a great-grandfather!"

Wes pointed toward Trevor with a broad laugh. "So is he, the old coot!"

A long table was set with a white table cloth in the backyard, only ten feet or so from their stretch of the beach. Long ago, Trevor and Kerry had called their property their "little slice of paradise." Even then, Kelli had known that their "slice" of paradise was a large piece. After all, they'd done very well in real estate and lived very comfortably in this large house, with its many rooms and its glorious view of the Vineyard Sound.

Dinner was served: burgers, grilled barbecue chicken, homemade fries, and potato salad— food perfect for a Fourth of July celebration. Prior to eating, Trevor stood to welcome everyone in a round of prayer.

"Dear Lord," he began as he closed his eyes. "Thank you for these tremendous gifts. When I look around the table at the Montgomery and Sheridan families, all together again, I comprehend the weight of all the time we spent apart, and I am so grateful for the time we have together now. Thank you, also, Oh Lord, for dear Beth, who has come into our lives and changed them forever. Her union with Andrew will bring us great joy— and, in the case of Andrew's mother, a great relief."

There was slight laughter at the table. Kelli didn't dare open her eyes to catch the perpetrator, although she suspected it was Audrey. Usually, when someone acted out, it was always Audrey.

Kelli was two seats away from Mark Van Tress. Between them sat her daughter, Lexi, while her other children, Josh and Sam, sat on the other side of the table. Amanda Harris and the other Sam, the manager of the Sunrise Cove, sat closer to her, but as the dishes were passed around, both Sam's hollered to one another, making jokes about having the same name.

"Now, you're Lexi, right?" Mark Van Tress asked as he scooped up some potato salad and placed it on his plate.

"That's right."

"And your mom is Kelli?"

"You got it again."

"Wow, and how old are you?"

"I just graduated from high school, and I work at the boutique for my mom right now since we're stretched thin. She works in real estate and owns the boutique."

Mark lifted his eyes toward Kelli's with curiosity. "A working woman. I'm impressed."

"I'm exhausted," Kelli joked. "But I don't have to tell you that. I'm sure you worked a full life yourself."

Mark gave a half-shrug. "But real estate. That's really something. You must know about all the properties in the Vineyard. Those of interest, anyway."

Kelli's cheeks burned the slightest bit with embarrassment. She didn't like being put on the spot at family gatherings and was normally grateful when the Sheridan sisters took the limelight.

"Oh, she's been trying to sell this crazy cool haunted hotel for a while now," Lexi interjected as she dove into the food before her.

"A haunted hotel? My, that's really something," Mark offered. "Where is it, may I ask?"

"It's to the southwest, along the edge of the cliffs," Kelli explained. "But the hotel was destroyed back in 1943. Nobody's touched it since, for some reason, even though the property is stunning. I'd love for someone to take over the place. Build it back up to what it once was. I hate going there and seeing all this potential every day, only to watch it continue to weather and rot. Another big storm and it might be gone for good."

Mark's look was curious. He tilted his head, then suggested, "My son and I have discussed opening a hotel on Martha's Vineyard for ages."

Kelli's heart began to patter in that way that had once

been familiar. Long ago, she had known what it meant to get excited about something. Was this that feeling? Was Mark Van Tress a potential buyer?

"What sort of hotel did you have in mind?"

"It would be something luxurious and most definitely a five-star hotel with a stunning view. The very sort of thing you're currently describing. And goodness, I love the historical background you're describing, minus the haunting aspect, of course." Mark rubbed his palms together conspiratorially.

"Sounds like you two should meet later," Trevor suggested across the table as he shifted his fork from left to right to point at the two of them on either side of Lexi.

"Let's make it a date, if that sounds all right with you," Mark stated firmly. His face transformed from his friendly, familial one to one of a businessman on the verge of a hugely rewarding opportunity.

Suddenly, Audrey clacked her fork against her wine glass. The others joined in, all eyes directed toward Beth and Andy. In response, they leaned in and kissed one another with their eyes closed, which resulted in whoops and hollers from all at the table.

"Goodness, don't they make the most beautiful couple?" Kerry cried.

Kelli searched her memories for her own pre-wedding times. Had Kerry said anything similar about Kelli and Mike? She couldn't remember now. She supposed it didn't matter at all.

Chapter Six

James liked Marilyn's hair a certain way. He had told her this on their wedding night, just before the Big Event had happened, and she'd felt belittled and youthful and silly in the wake of it, as though, at first, he had to insult her appearance before he then took one of the most important things from her: her virginity. Being a woman seemed endlessly cruel.

They had been at the Aquinnah Cliffs Overlook Hotel for three days now. Marilyn sat on the stool in front of the round mirror in the presidential suite and prepared her hair just so, in the style that ensured James wouldn't have a hissy fit before dinner. For not the first time, she wondered what sort of man he would be like when they finally had children. She knew in her heart that it wouldn't be easy, but nothing ever was.

James bustled through the room just as she finished her half-up-do. He'd spent the afternoon riding with Robert, assessing him. He hadn't yet broken the news that he wanted to buy his hotel; rather, he was hunting him, monitoring his prey until the perfect time to strike. This wasn't the first time in their very young marriage that Marilyn had watched him perform just this action. It disgusted her, but it also enthralled her. She was married to perhaps an evil man. How infinitely unlucky she was!

"Darling, how did it go?" She asked because she knew that if she didn't, James would demand why she hadn't.

"Oh, fine." He sounded flippant. "The man is difficult to read. He did take me on a splendorous ride. It's such a beautiful island, Marilyn. You really must ride with me next time. You're a rather strong rider."

Rather strong? It was an insult to Marilyn, who'd spent her entire youth on a horse. It was the country girl's way. Even still, it was about as great of a compliment that James Peterson could give.

"Are you ready for dinner, darling?" Marilyn stood and placed a strained kiss on her husband's cheek. "I'm sure you're quite hungry."

This would be the sort of dialogue she'd have for the rest of her life. *Are you hungry? Are you thirsty? Am I meeting your needs in bed?* Forever, into eternity, until hopefully, one of them died early. She didn't mind who.

They dressed in their dinnertime best and walked down the grand staircase toward the ballroom below. The restaurant was attached to the ballroom, but it was still too early for any sort of dance. The ceiling had been painted beautifully; it was reminiscent of photos and drawings Marilyn had studied of ceilings in Italy. Her heart surged with excitement for the details of the place. Suppose James did buy it? Perhaps she could spend her days in the presidential suite, walking the coast, while James wandered the globe, buying up whatever he could. If he wrote her letters — imagine him ever writing a letter! — she would ignore them.

A Vineyard Rebirth

Maybe she would take a lover.

Ah, but no. She couldn't think like that. The only people who were happy in the prison they lived in were the ones who could imagine it wasn't such a cage. She had to be creative.

James and Marilyn sat at their now-familiar table near the window with its endless, gorgeous view of the bluffs. A waiter arrived promptly to pour them glasses of red wine. Marilyn was happy to dull her senses before James blathered on.

"I feel this place isn't properly managed, Marilyn." James leaned across the table and furrowed his brow. He looked excitable, like a teenager on the brink of revolt. "I don't think this Robert character knows what he's doing. He says he understands the very core of hospitality and that this place kind of fell in his lap after some man named Johnson passed it on to him, but I'm not so sure. He says it was a whirlwind, figuring out what to do with it and how to manage it. I mentioned already— well, that it sounds like he needs some help! But his face was difficult to read."

"I see." She folded her hands gently on her lap.

The food arrived a moment later. James looked tipsier than normal, as though all the riding had wiped him out. He dove into his piece of quail, his motions swift, while Marilyn ate slowly, studying him. As he also drank quickly, he grew increasingly drunk and didn't notice her constant watch.

"Robert, my boy!" James lifted a hand as Robert Sheridan stepped into the dining room.

It seemed to Marilyn that the string quintet in the corner actually faltered as a result of James' wild screech. Her heart started to race at the idea. How embarrassing.

But Robert didn't miss a beat. He took a few steps toward their table, bowed his head in greeting, and said, "I trust your dinner serves you well?"

"Very well, Mr. Sheridan," Marilyn murmured. Slowly, her heart began to climb into her throat as her eyes found his seafoam green ones. What was it about this man? Why did she yearn to wrap her arms around him and cry?

"I've told you. Please, call me Robert." His smile didn't falter, not once.

"The meal is a delight, Robert. But please. Sit with us for a moment, won't you? I suppose I didn't quite get enough during our outing this afternoon."

There was silence for a split second. Marilyn sensed that Robert knew James was quite drunk. Even still, he wasn't the sort to embarrass James. He grabbed a chair from an empty table and placed it between the two of them. A waiter quickly brought him a wine glass, which was soon filled with the restaurant's best.

"Must be marvelous to own this place," James commented, leaning back in his chair before continuing. "As much of that delightful French wine as they can pour for you." He slurred his words. Marilyn's stomach burned with embarrassment.

Suppose Robert thought Marilyn had actually chosen this man to marry. On purpose? How wretched.

"It's truly a wonderful thing," Robert said as he studied this increasingly drunken man before him.

James lifted the bottle of wine and poured himself another hearty glass. He lifted it so that the wine within sparkled with the light from the chandelier. "Here's to you, Robert Sheridan. To you and your beautiful hotel and all those who come from miles around to reside in it."

Robert arched an eyebrow but played along. He clinked his glass with James', then turned his gaze toward Marilyn. He seemed inquisitive.

"I don't suppose you'd ever want to depart from this island?" James asked after he sipped. "Run off to some other golden shores elsewhere. Make something of yourself in the city." He leaned closer to Robert, his eyes sparkling. "You should see the women in the city, Rob. About as pretty as they get, I reckon."

"Is that so?" Robert cocked an eyebrow. He was making fun of him with just the tone of his voice.

Marilyn's stomach felt filled with stones. She'd long since supposed that James cheated on her. Perhaps this was his admittance— and right in front of her! He didn't care; why would he? Her parents had given her away to him; it had been an agreement, a trade. She felt like nothing. And certainly, she wasn't a city girl.

"Seriously, Robert. You wouldn't have to marry them. They're loose and wild and free down there. You could have your pick, a handsome man like you. Wouldn't they be all over him, Marilyn? Huh?"

Marilyn was caught off-guard. She sniffed, then gave a half-nod.

"She's always like that. So quiet," James said. He showed his teeth horribly. "But in any case. I shouldn't beat around the bush. I hate when other men do that, and thusly, I won't do it to you. I want to purchase your hotel, Robert. I want it so bad that I'm willing to lay down my life for it."

Robert laughed outright. "Lay down your life?"

"It's just a dramatic expression, Rob."

Robert crossed his arms over his chest. James took another enormous sip of wine and nearly tumbled from his chair. Marilyn leaped up and reached for him, but he swatted her away, anger marring his face. The impact stung.

Robert knew better than to say something. Still, his eyes told his true feelings: he was enraged that James had swatted her. Marilyn steadied James as he stood. He slurred, "If you'll excuse me, I must speak to my wife in private." Marilyn then directed them both toward the staircase, where they sauntered up to the top level. She had to drag him half the way. When they reached the presidential suite, she pressed her hands against his chest, and he fell onto the bed. In a split second, he fell fast asleep. How much had he drunk? The entire bottle in thirty minutes flat?

Marilyn steadied herself. She reached for a bottle of wine he'd brought into the room earlier and drank directly from the bottle to steady her nerves. She then peered at herself in the mirror. What did anyone see when they viewed her? She was just James Peterson's arm candy, she supposed— nothing more. At least that's how he made her feel.

She reached up and removed the little clips in her hair, the ones that caught the locks in the half-up, half-down hairdo that James liked so much. When her hair was freed, she whipped it around so that it grew wild and untamed and, in her mind, more beautiful. She then turned and headed for the door, careful to keep her footfalls light. When she reached the hallway, her stomach grew tense with horror. What was she doing? What was she headed toward?

But in a flash, she was downstairs again. She returned to the table she had shared with both men, only to find it void of Robert. She sat anyway and poured herself a hefty drink. She needed it after that embarrassing display.

It didn't take long for Robert to reappear. He stopped short at her table and looked at the empty chair across from her.

"I suppose James couldn't make it back to dinner."

"He's indisposed, I'm afraid."

"Regrettable." He replied as though he'd never heard anything happier in his life.

"Indeed."

There was a moment of silence. Marilyn sipped her drink, then told herself not to drink too quickly and wind up as drunk as her husband.

"May I sit with you for a moment?"

Marilyn's throat grew thick with tension. "Of course."

He sat in James' old chair. She felt she'd never seen anyone more handsome.

"I like what you've done with your hair. I hope that isn't too forward to say."

Marilyn blinked at him. He didn't know that this was the perfect thing to say. Or did he somehow sense it?

"Thank you. I suppose it isn't the most proper way."

"Screw propriety," Robert returned, flashing her a genuine smile.

Marilyn's lips parted. He spoke differently than most men. He spoke without airs. Perhaps this was due to his islander roots. He had nothing of the city-boy mentality. Thank goodness.

"Tell me. What do you think of Martha's Vineyard?"

"I suppose my husband has already said what we think. We think it's beautiful. So beautiful that he'd like to buy your hotel."

"But I want to know what you think." He pointed toward her as he leaned into the table.

Marilyn hadn't been asked what she thought in what seemed like years. It struck her as bizarre. Naturally, her own thoughts stirred around her mind non-stop. She'd long since put up a barrier between her brain and her mouth to ensure nothing slipped through. Who deserved her actual opinions? Almost no one.

But maybe Robert did.

"I think it's one of the most magical places I've ever been to," she murmured with so much truth. "I've been captivated with the property since the very first day. I feel something in the air—a promise of something I can't possibly describe. Perhaps my husband feels it too; maybe this is why he is so hungry to buy your hotel. But he doesn't have a particularly poetic soul, so perhaps I'm putting something within him that doesn't exist."

Robert's eyes glowed with the light from the chandelier. Marilyn wondered what it might be like to kiss him. She'd read books of women who had affairs; always, they ended in tragedy. She had never imagined herself to be that sort of woman.

But didn't she want to operate in a world of endless romance and beauty?

They continued to speak. Robert leaned toward her with each of her sentences, seeming to take stock in what she said and how she said it. James hadn't listened to her in ages, and Marilyn found herself addicted to this attention. He never once removed his gaze from her eyes. Once or twice, she actually wondered if he saw her body at all—if he appreciated it. She immediately felt shame for this feeling. She couldn't allow herself to go down this road.

When the bottle of wine was finished, Robert ordered

A Vineyard Rebirth

them another, one from Italy. Marilyn ached for him to take her hand and take her away, perhaps to his private quarters. Instead, she asked him about his background. His parents owned an inn in Oak Bluffs; he'd wanted something grander, something with more magic. He'd been given the old hotel because he'd grown close to the old man who had owned it previously. "I did odd jobs for him around here. He spoke to me about the great loves and losses of his life. He was terribly sad and terribly lonely. When he left this world, he left the hotel to me. I couldn't understand it— but I wanted to honor it with everything I had. I knew that would be the most important thing to him."

"And here you are—honoring it. It's really beautiful."

"I don't always know if that's true," he returned with a little jump to his shoulder. "I've certainly put a lot of my time into the place. Perhaps that's enough."

"Isn't time really the only resource?" Marilyn asked. It was something she'd thought about endlessly.

Robert's grin widened. He sipped his wine, then said, "I knew it."

Marilyn furrowed her brow. "What? Please tell me what you know?"

"I knew you were smarter than him. Much, much smarter."

Marilyn's stomach tightened again. "I don't know what you mean."

"You do. And perhaps you'll pretend you don't till your dying day, but you'll always know what I mean."

Marilyn turned her gaze to her newly-poured glass of wine. She'd grown foggy with the alcohol, but she rather liked this feeling— as though she'd left the rest of the world behind.

"Are you from the city as well?" he asked her then.

It had been years, as well, since anyone had asked her a question about herself.

"I'm not. I'm from a tiny town in upstate New York," she told him.

"You must miss it."

"Why do you say that?"

"I've only been to the city a few times, but it's stifling," Robert admitted. "Especially if you're used to the clean air and the quiet."

"And the stars," Marilyn breathed, turning to look out at the view. "I miss the stars."

Robert's smile faltered. "You need them back."

Marilyn chuckled. "They're here, at least. I have them here for now. Until you kick my husband and me to the curb and tell him you'll never sell, which you should do, by the way. Tell him that because he doesn't deserve such a beautiful place." She covered her mouth as quickly as the words fell and then whispered, "I've said too much."

"You've said too little, in my opinion." Robert poured another drink, then leaned forward with a display of curiosity etched across his face. "Tell me, Marilyn, if I may call you that."

"You may. But only here." All the tables around them had cleared out. She didn't dare look at the clock on the wall to know the time. She knew it had to be near midnight or well past. If James knew what she was up to, she was doomed.

But more than likely, he was still dead to the world.

"All right." Robert placed his fingers around the wine stem and moved the glass around timidly. He needed time, maybe, to build up confidence. "Tell me why you married him."

A Vineyard Rebirth

Marilyn felt it: the sinister hatred behind his words. Her throat tightened.

"It was an arranged marriage my father made a long time ago."

Robert's eyes grew shadowed. "That's wretched."

"We were poor. We were always so poor, and he had me to offer. I suppose my siblings and parents are doing quite well now. I can take solace in that."

"But you're a prisoner."

"A prisoner who drinks fine wine, eats fine meals, and stays in luxury hotels on the coastline," she pointed out. "It isn't so bad, is it?"

"But you miss the stars."

Marilyn's heart felt squeezed. "I hope you won't mention to James that I told you all this."

"I don't suppose he'd take it well."

Marilyn dropped her gaze to the table. "I wish I could love him. It would be easier."

She immediately regretted her words. It was too much. But in a flash, Robert splayed his hand over hers, there on the table. It stayed there for only a split second before he removed it. Marilyn thought she would remember the sensation of his skin upon hers for the rest of her life.

"I had better get to bed," she whispered. "Thank you for the wonderful conversation. You must understand—it's nothing I'm accustomed to."

"But you must have had these sorts of conversations before."

"Yes, with my father."

She could see that his troubled Robert all the more. "And he still gave you over to James?"

Marilyn could feel her tears threaten to fall. She willed them to wait till she returned to her room.

"He explained that this is a man's world. I was born into it and I will die out of it. Till then, I must do as he and my husband say." She took a final sip of wine and felt her head cloud all the more.

"I don't mean any harm, but your father sounds cruel."

"He's a realist, as I must be. Goodnight, Robert Sheridan. I will see you soon."

Marilyn walked all the way up to the presidential suite with her ears ringing wildly. When she reached the other side of the door, she slid down it as the sound of James's snores rattled from wall to wall. She pressed her hands together over her heart and dared for a moment to dream of another reality.

But of course, she knew better than all that.

Chapter Seven

"You can only do so much when they're adults. I taught him everything I could. Tardiness is not to be tolerated." Mark Van Tress's eyes sparkled with the joke. He sat in the front room of Kelli's real estate office, a can of sparkling water in hand and one very expensive shoe placed delicately across his knee. He and Kelli had been waiting for the arrival of his son, Xander Van Tress, for nearly twenty minutes. He was a developer with more money than God, apparently, with recent projects in Nantucket and an island off the coast of Seattle.

"I understand." Kelli flashed him a smile. "My children are grown up these days. I have to admit; I don't think I instilled in them every life lesson I could have."

"Ah, well. At the end of the day, I suppose we are only human."

"Isn't that a tragedy?" Kelli laughed. "How I longed for perfection back in the old days. I thought I would have achieved it by now."

The bell from the front door rang as a stranger

entered. The man was in his late forties, a sort of rugged Brad Pitt type, during the shaggier era. Kelli's heart stopped beating for a split second before it cranked up again. She stood up as the man gave her a delicious, crooked grin.

"There he is. The man of the hour." Mark stood and greeted his son with a firm nod.

"My ferry was a few minutes late," Xander Van Tress explained, taking a few strides forward. His eyes remained locked on Kelli's.

She was unaccustomed to any sort of attention from men. Not like she'd put herself out there since Mike's departure, but even still. Once you were a woman of a certain age— it's not like that attention came your way any longer. Unless you were a Sheridan sister, that is.

She quickly told herself that his attention was all business-related. After all, he potentially wanted to buy the property on the cliffside. She built up a boundary around her heart to fight off any kind of disappointment. So many others had come before these men. Still, the property remained barren.

"I'm Kelli. Kelli Montgomery," she greeted brightly, in that real-estate tone she'd taken on several years before — the one that rang false and strange in her own ears. She shook Xander's hand firmly.

"Good to meet you." Xander smiled. "My father has told me a great deal already about this property. It sounds right up our alley. I've had dreams about something like this. A kind of mystical, haunted land with a story of its own."

Kelli's heart twitched. "I see you're a dreamer."

"It's the reason I got into all of this developer stuff," he told her. "I wanted to make these dreams come to life.

There's something about the air of a place, of a piece of land— an aura, maybe, if you want to get esoteric about it. I feel it in my bones, and then I try to build a place with that aura in mind. In this way, my properties are known to be incredibly diverse."

"It's true. There's no way like the Van Tress way," Mark affirmed. "My son is quite taken with the multitudes of paths that architecture allows."

Again, Kelli was reminded of those blueprints, which she wanted to take to the antiquarian to investigate further. If her hunch about the blueprints was correct, and the Van Tress father-son duo really went forward with this project, those blueprints would come in handy. She had a hunch that Xander was the sort of man to appreciate them.

Or perhaps she'd already given him too much credit, simply due to the handsomeness of his face, his square chin, the broadness of his chest, and that unique cologne he wore— was it sandalwood? Her heart felt squeezed.

"Shall we drive to the property, then?"

They made their way outside. Mark jumped in the back of her vehicle to allow Xander space in front. Kelli was self-conscious about everything. The radio DJ played an obnoxious number of commercials during the first five minutes of their route, and she found herself apologizing, as though she'd planned the schedule herself.

"Nothing like capitalism, huh?" Xander joked.

At this, Kelli let out a laugh that sounded a bit too nervous for her liking. She again cursed herself. But what did it mean to flirt, anyway? How had she scored Mike? Then again, her instincts had obviously been horrific in that case. Could she even trust herself?

Xander stood with his feet shoulder-width apart and

his hands on his hips. The July sunlight cascaded beautifully across his dark blond beard, and his blue eyes scanned the property, the craggy cliffside, and then the mansion itself, or what was left of it. Kelli was captivated by his captivation; she sensed in a flash that he was truly mesmerized by the old place. He heard its song.

"1943, huh?"

"The year of the hurricane," she affirmed. "It was devastating."

Xander's steps were long and confident. He strode forward without her, something the other potential buyers had never done, and headed directly toward what was left of the front door. He peered through the shadows. Kelli walked up the stone staircase behind him and followed his gaze. The foyer's marble floors were cracked but still very much intact, proof of the immaculate state of the old place.

"I wish I could see that old ballroom," he said. "It disappears beneath that rubble."

"The ceiling was beautifully painted," Kelli stated. "I can show you an old photograph if you like."

"If we did rebuild this back up, we would need to reinstate something like that," Xander said thoughtfully. "Hire a classical painter."

"It could take forever."

Xander's eyes were stoic. "Good things take time."

Kelli tilted her head as they held one another's gaze.

"You look as though you've never heard that expression before." Xander turned to face her, a puzzled look etched across his face.

Kelli's laugh was quiet, nearly lost to the whipping winds there on the cliffside. "It's just that spending a lot of time on details isn't necessarily something most developers bother with. In my experience, it's all money-money-money, into infinity."

Xander shrugged. "I have money. I've had money for years. Now, I work on passion projects. The money is a wonderful benefit of all the hard work and thought I put into them. But it's not my primary mission. I think the guests eventually find that they feel that difference, as well. But who knows when this place will ultimately open again? It could take two years, or it could take five."

Kelli's heart pattered with excitement. She was reminded of learning about old paintings that had taken years to paint, of books that had taken the writer fifteen years to research and scribe. Good things really did take time—ten months to form a baby. Perhaps a year or so to build a trustful love with someone. It was refreshing to meet a man who understood this.

It had not taken long for her and Mike to unravel their world.

"Maybe if I were a younger man, I would step on through that doorway and try to get as far in as I could," Xander told her as he gestured toward the doorway.

"Please, don't." Kelli laughed. "It was a hang-out place in the sixties— hippies smoking pot and all that. I think they loved the magic of the place the way we do. They felt it in the air. But one guy went all the way up to the tower and fell. Apparently, it wasn't a pretty sight."

Xander lifted his chin to gaze up at the top of the tower. "Imagine being a hippie in the sixties, high out of your mind, and climbing up there. He must have felt on top of the world, if only for a moment."

Kelli chuckled. She'd never in her life tried pot. Had Xander? Was she a square not to have branched out, tried new things? Mike was the only man she had ever been with. She suddenly second-guessed everything.

Xander stepped down from the stone staircase to meet his father at the base of it. He muttered something to Mark, too soft for Kelli to hear. She drew a curl around her ear. Was this the moment when Xander would go back on everything he'd just said? Should she have not told him about the tower and the hippie's fall?

"It's really something," Mark said to her then. "You said you had old photographs of the place when it was up and running, right?"

Kelli snapped her fingers. "Of course, I'll grab them now." She hustled toward the car and grabbed the manilla folder, which was filled with print-outs Brittany had found online. She splayed the folder open on the hood of the car as Mike and Xander gathered on either side of her.

"The photos are a bit earlier, from the twenties," she explained as she held them out for both to see. "But you can see the state of the place. Absolutely beautiful, wasn't it? And look at those outfits."

The late twenties had been a joyous time on the island. In many of the photographs, women and men played croquet together and drank cocktails beneath the sunlight. Men were serious in the photographs; their mustaches were thick and swept down on either side of their mouths. Several of the women, though, had been captured mid-laughter. In one photo, an older gentleman stood on the cliffside. According to the article online, this man owned the hotel at the time. A man named Johnson.

"And here are photos of the ballroom," Kelli pointed. "They aren't crystal clear, but you can get a sense for the

A Vineyard Rebirth

grandness of the ceiling and the restaurant, which was attached."

Xander whistled. He lifted the photo and squinted his eyes to try to glean every last detail. "I wonder why people lost interest in these kinds of designs."

"I guess it again comes down to personal taste and money," Kelli returned.

Mark and Xander exchanged glances. Xander placed the photos together again in the manilla envelope.

"Would you mind if we take these along with us?"

"Of course not. I can always print more."

"Thank you."

Another breeze ripped past them. Xander laughed as his hair fluttered around him. He turned back to catch a last glimpse of the place.

"That wind is strong up here. No wonder the old place fell apart during a hurricane," he said. "I'm about to fall apart myself."

After a walk around the property itself, Kelli, Mark, and Xander returned to the car. Xander announced that he and his father had a great deal to discuss in the wake of this viewing but that they were infinitely intrigued. Kelli didn't dare get her hopes up. She stepped on the gas and drove them back to Oak Bluffs as, thankfully, the radio DJ played music that made the air bright and optimistic.

"I love this one," Xander said of a tune by Electric Light Orchestra. "Makes me think of long car rides with my old dad."

"Who you calling old?" Mark chuckled from the back seat. "Kelli, we used to run around this continent together, me and Xander here. We didn't have two nickels to rub together, but we always found a way to pay for gas."

"We were very resourceful back then," Xander admitted. "But all that travel gave me a real appreciation for a number of things. For the culture and the history of this great country. And, of course, for the value of money."

"Sounds like you two were like the male version of Thelma and Louise," Kelli said, giving Xander a sideways glance.

Mark and Xander laughed outright. Mark smacked his knee.

"You're really something, Kelli. You remind me of Trevor and Wes. They were always mischievous. Always had something up their sleeves, with more brains than they should have been allowed."

Kelli had never thought of herself as particularly clever or funny, especially when compared to her brothers and sisters or her cousins. For the first time, she wondered if she'd been bred to think that way about herself as a result of living out her days with Mike.

Maybe she could overcome it.

Back at the real estate office, Mark shook her hand and thanked her again. He began to strut off back to his vehicle while Xander hovered by hers for a moment. Again, Kelli thought this was Xander, making time to tell her he actually wasn't interested in the property without embarrassing her in front of his dad.

But instead, he said, "That property and the way you talk about it— it's really something special, Kelli. I have this feeling that you have a number of things to say, all of them interesting and all of them good."

Kelli's cheeks flushed. What was happening?

"I would really like to take you out for a drink and pick your brain," he continued. "I wonder if you'd be up for that."

"I'm not sure my brain is in season," Kelli returned. "Is this business or pleasure?"

Xander chuckled. "Don't worry about that. Just say you will."

Kelli's voice crackled. "Why should I?"

Xander shrugged. "If you don't, I'll be disappointed. And all I am is a simple man. I hate being disappointed. I suppose there will be no consequences besides that. The earth won't shift on its axis. The sun will continue to rise and fall. And we will continue to lead our separate lives."

Kelli's eyes sparkled for just a brief moment. She hadn't been asked out on a date since her teenage years. Even though she knew it would be mostly about work, she could see that he may be interested in her as well. It made her body tingle with excitement.

"Okay, I'm up for it, but only because I can't bear to see a grown man disappointed."

Xander's laughter was like music to her ears. "Then I'll be in contact. You won't regret it." He then turned on his heel and headed for his father, who gave him a curious smile. They were like two peas in a pod, with history and texture between them to fill multiple storybooks. Kelli's heart surged with intrigue.

What on earth would happen next?

Chapter Eight

The old antiquarian had a little cottage tucked into the forest around Oak Bluffs. His name was Frederick Bachman, and as was fitting, he was something of a loner, frequently keeping to himself, tinkering with his very old things and paying no mind to the outside world or the present day. He made his money with his sought-after goods, the likes of which people came to the Vineyard to purchase for upwards of hundreds of thousands of dollars. He had an eye for detail and could fix nearly anything up to its previous state.

Kelli had never met Frederick Bachman before. Prior to her arrival with the blueprints, she spoke to him over the phone. His voice was raspy and deep, like something he didn't use very often. He told her to come in the late afternoon, after his nap. He didn't seem to regret telling her this very personal detail. She wondered if he took pleasure in telling her something so intimate— as she was sure he didn't tell anyone very much, if anything at all.

"Would you like me to bring you anything?" she

asked, as he was a recluse and probably didn't appreciate tasks like going to the store.

"Oh, no. I have a young man do all my shopping for me every Monday," Frederick replied. "I'm all set."

The cottage was like something out of a storybook. Kelli took a deep breath outside of it, then stepped lightly up the little stone pathway toward the bright red front door. She clacked the golden knocker and waited until she heard the shuffling of feet.

The man who opened the door couldn't have been more than five feet tall. He was slumped over, his shoulders hunched, proof that he had spent his life at a desk studying very old antiques and many other things. It was as though his back wanted to prepare the rest of his body for what was to come, like something to be studied down the line by the next person. Of course, it seemed a rarer thing these days that anyone was curious about old things at all.

This was one of the first things Frederick told Kelli as he took the blueprints. "People simply don't care anymore. They just throw things away without giving it a second thought. Years and years of history gone. I'm the only one left to try to pick up the pieces."

His workshop was an unorganized yet fascinating space. Everywhere you looked, there was something to cling to— an old cuckoo clock, which he said had been made in Germany and brought to the Vineyard in the forties; a collection of jewelry items from eighteenth-century England; an old rocking horse built in the year 1911; and the list went on. Kelli was terrified to break anything. She hovered in the doorway and watched as Frederick placed the rolled-up blueprint center stage on his desk.

"Do you have a hunch of what it might be for?"

She nodded delicately. "I think they're for the old Aquinnah Cliffside Overlook Hotel."

Shock crept across his face. "The old Overlook? You don't say."

Kelli nodded. "It's not a total surprise it would be in my parents' attic. They've been in charge of the sale for as long as I can remember."

"Fascinating." Frederick's face was now a flurry of activity. "It appears to have quite the water damage. I'm glad you brought it to me without trying to unroll it yourself. These things must be handled delicately. And, as I'm sure you know, the hotel was built in the early 1800s. Long, long ago."

"I'm very familiar and was terrified to have such a beautiful thing in my possession. I hope you can bring it to life again."

"It's not a matter of hoping, my dear." He slid his small round glasses up his nose. "It's just a matter of patience. I will show you these blueprints— but it will take me time."

"I have time," Kelli told him, remembering again what Xander had said about good things and what they needed to survive.

Kelli gave the man her number and bid him goodbye. She left with regret as she ached to remain in that space a little bit longer, breathing in the gritty air of the previous eras that lingered there. In many ways, Frederick himself was a relic of a previous era. How she longed to ask him about his own stories and what had led him to be a recluse. In truth, she could imagine a similar reality for herself— tucked away on her own somewhere with her books, hiding away from the world.

No. She'd had children. They wouldn't allow her a hiding place.

And wasn't that part of the reason people had children, somehow? To ensure they didn't wind up all alone?

* * *

Susan had invited her female cousins and sisters, along with the next generation of women, over to her new house for dinner and drinks. After she dropped off the blueprints, Kelli directed her car over to the "Sheridan Estate," which now consisted of the original family home and the home directly beside it, which Scott had purchased and built back up with the help of his teenage son. Kelli hadn't had much contact with the son but had heard about his trouble at school, which had led to his moving to the Vineyard full-time. This hadn't been something Susan had prepared for in the wake of her reunion with Scott. Kelli couldn't imagine she would have handled it well— having to parent a teenage boy with barely any notice at all. Still, Susan Sheridan could do anything. She was a superhero.

Lexi pulled up just a split second after Kelli arrived. Audrey sat in her front seat and gave a little wave. Kelli hadn't known that the girls had begun to spend time together. Lexi jumped out and gave her mother a hug. "Audrey stopped into the boutique today, and we just got to chatting," she explained.

Audrey lifted Max's little baby carrier from the backseat and carried it delicately. "I just love some of the clothes you have in that little store. It's beautiful! And finally, my body feels ready to slip back into clothing I actually like." She turned her eyes toward the sleeping baby and cooed, "It's all your fault, isn't it, Baby Max? Huh?"

Kelli chuckled. She'd heard the Sheridan sisters discussing the fact that Audrey had returned to what seemed like her pre-baby body in no time flat. This was the nature of a twenty-year-old's body, she supposed.

"Look at this place," Lexi breathed as she lifted her chin toward the large house.

"I know. Aunt Susan really nabbed a great guy," Audrey affirmed. "Not many of us meet the love of our lives when we're a teenager. But she's a forward-thinker, our Sue."

Claire and Charlotte pulled up after that. In the back seat sat Kelli's nieces— Rachel, Gail, and Abby, all of whom were absolute best friends. Gail and Abby were sixteen-year-old twins and the daughters of Claire and her husband, Russell, while Rachel was Charlotte's fifteen-year-old daughter with her now-deceased husband, who she'd lost in a tragic fishing accident years before. The previous November, she'd met a photographer, Everett, at the iconic and forever-memorable wedding for Ursula Pennington, the actress. The three weeks she'd taken to plan it was burned in Kelli's memory forever. Throughout, Mike had tried to make bets that she wouldn't pull it off in time. Kelli had resisted, praying only for her baby sister to throw it all together at the last second. And dammit, she had. She was now one of the most talked-about wedding planners from coast to coast. *Take that, Mike.*

They found Christine, Susan, Amanda, and Lola already on the back porch, with a gorgeous view of the Vineyard Sound and several opened bottles of wine between them. Christine glowed from her pregnancy and sipped sparkling water with lemon. Lola bucked up, a bright bolt of energy, and grabbed several more chairs from the side of the porch, arranging them so that everyone else could sit.

"Mom should be here shortly," Claire explained. "She wanted to bring clam chowder."

"Goodness. She didn't have to do that! I thought we'd just order pizza," Susan exclaimed.

"You know Mom. She always wants to help out. Especially when it comes to the Sheridans," Charlotte affirmed. She lifted a bottle and filled a glass for herself, then one for Claire and Kelli. Rachel disappeared and reappeared with cans of sodas for her and the other girls. Although only twenty, Audrey arched an eyebrow and poured herself a glass of wine without pause.

"Well, we appreciate her. Always have," Christine admitted.

Kelli excused herself for a moment for the bathroom. Down the hallway, there was an old photograph of Anna Sheridan, the Sheridan sisters' mother, who'd passed away many years before. Kelli remembered the bright light of her gorgeous Aunt Anna. She had been endlessly energetic, much like Lola, with all of the beauty of the three of them somehow combined in one. Her and Wes's at-times tumultuous marriage and endless commitment to the Sunrise Cove Inn had led her to stray from their marriage and sleep with Stan Ellis, something of a loner on the island. Stan Ellis had been the man behind the wheel of the boat that had crashed the night Anna died. Lola had been eleven, Christine fourteen, and Susan seventeen. Kelli supposed they would never get over it—and it was the reason Kerry was now late, as she still felt she had to be the mother figure for those poor motherless girls.

Kelli studied herself in the mirror of the bathroom. The mirror itself was a very special antique, that much was clear, and she made a mental note to ask Susan where she'd picked it up. Kelli now considered her own house and how all of the items in it had been hand-selected by Kelli and Mike as a couple. What might she have chosen had she been alone?

Was it possible to give it all away and start over?

When Kelli left the bathroom, she found Susan and Charlotte in the kitchen. Susan described the elaborate work Scott and his son had done over the months leading up to their wedding. She beamed as she pointed out each delicate touch and the fine craftsmanship.

"Everett and I have discussed building a place of our own," Charlotte admitted. "Rachel is a bit hesitant about moving out of the place we shared with her dad, but I think it would be a good fresh start for all of us."

Kelli remembered that it had taken Charlotte years to even get rid of her husband's shirts in the wake of his accident. Her house had operated as a kind of shrine to his memory. Kelli, Kerry, and Claire had fallen into non-stop conversation about what to do about Charlotte. It turned out the answer had fallen onto Everett's shoulders instead.

"Some of the decor you picked is just stunning, Susan," Kelli said, leaning up against the wall. "Did you find yourself drawn to a different style this time, as you built up a home with a different man?"

The question was personal, but Susan took it in stride. Honesty was her policy. Kelli appreciated this so much about her.

"Yes. With Richard, I chose everything with the idea that we had to represent ourselves as confident, intelligent attorneys. Nothing could be chosen for the artistry of it; it had to be designer or state-of-the-art. If I didn't receive at least four compliments on any given dinner occasion, I deemed myself a failure and bought something new. It was intense, to say the least." Susan spread her hands out toward the living room and the grand stone fireplace, which Scott and Kellan had built themselves. "But this place represents my soul. I feel Scott's love for me in every room. And I purchased the furnishings and the art with our love in mind. Don't get me wrong; I loved my home in Newark. But this place? It seems connected to me in ways I couldn't have dreamed of before. I'm so grateful."

Chapter Nine

"I just eat up this story about the hotel." Lola hovered near Kelli with her wine glass lifted, her voice low and mischievous. "All that romance. All that horror. I mean, I remember stories about it when we were growing up, that it was haunted. I always begged Susan to drive Christine and I over there when she got her driver's license, but she wouldn't."

"What wouldn't I do?" Susan called as she whipped past before she popped a cookie in her mouth. It was one of Christine's specialties— a chocolate macadamia gooey masterpiece.

"You would never have any fun," Lola hollered.

"Fun? Aunt Susan? She's never heard of it," Audrey piped up from the doorway. Max had begun to whimper, and she again propped him in the little wrap around her chest and bobbed him lightly so that her knees popped out and back in.

"Oh, you. I've had my share. Maybe too much," Susan said after she swallowed her cookie bite.

"Your idea of fun is chasing after a good case," Christine pointed out as she rubbed her pregnant belly. "One time, I asked you what kind of hobbies you wanted to take up when you had more time after your divorce and you said, maybe volunteer more for people in need. You put Mother Theresa to shame."

"Anyway, Tommy and I went out to the property last week," Lola continued as she returned her gaze to Kelli. "And I took some really spectacular shots of the place. It was on that foggy day before it kicked up a rain."

"Oh! Show me."

Lola pulled out her phone and searched through her online folders until she found her rather professional-looking photography. As she flipped through, she explained that she'd had to get to some level with her photography skills, as she often didn't have a photographer on hand as a journalist.

"It's better if you can do both if you need to," she explained. Her eyes shot toward Audrey, who continued to bob Max near the wall.

"I'm listening, dear mother," Audrey teased.

"That's right. You're headed back to school this fall to study journalism, aren't you?" Kelli asked then, wording it as delicately as she could. She wasn't entirely sure how a young woman could possibly leave her baby behind. Probably, the event would crack her heart in two. Still, this had been the arrangement since the beginning, with Christine and her fiancé, Zach, taking over the responsibility.

"That's the plan," Audrey recited, her voice heavy with doubt.

"Anyway. These photos, along with the story you told, got me thinking," Lola said. "I would love to write a piece about it. Dig into the grittier details about the hurricane and interview people on the island who might still be around. I mean, 1943 was a long time ago, but it's not like it's so ancient of history, you know? I'm sure there are many residents on the island who hold some kind of connection."

This had never occurred to Kelli. She gave a slight shrug and then added, "I actually have a potential buyer, if you can believe it."

"Oh gosh. Do you think the buyer will uphold the artistic heritage of the place?" Lola asked as a wrinkle formed between her brows.

The image of Xander Van Tress on the top of that small stone staircase, peering into the darkness of the dilapidated ballroom, sprung to Kelli's mind. She nodded slowly. "I do, actually. And Mom and I might have discovered the old blueprints in the attic. I have an antiquarian looking over them now. I don't think it'll be too hard to convince Xan— I mean, Mr. Van Tress, to take stock in them. Maybe he could merge the new with the old."

Lola nodded with excitement. "This should all go in the article. Maybe I could pick your brain about this sometime later when we aren't all fuzzy with wine. What do you say?"

Kelli's heart lightened. Things seemed to be in transition. People were interested in what she did; people genuinely cared about her, even in the wake of the horror of her divorce. Her opinion of herself had been below ground level. Slowly, it was rising to back to a normal status.

"I would love that."

* * *

A Vineyard Rebirth

The article about the Aquinnah Cliffside Overlook Hotel and its potential purchase was published in an online magazine based in Boston later that week. Kelli was surprised at the swift turn-around time, but Lola explained that she wanted the thing up and running before the hotel was actually sold.

"Maybe this will make your buyer have a bit more competition and raise his price," she pointed out over the phone.

Kelli tore through the article again, genuinely impressed with Lola's way with words. She discussed the dramatic history of the old place, the way it had transformed the island during the years directly after the whaling boom, and how, with the hurricane of 1943, the landscape of the island and where the tourists had flocked and celebrated in the summertime months had shifted. Lola had even tracked down an old man named Dexter Collington, who'd worked alongside his father at the Aquinnah Cliffside Overlook Hotel during his youth prior to the destruction of the place.

"It was just about the most magical place I'd ever seen," Dexter stated in the article. "My father would wake me up an hour before the crack of dawn so we could race over to the cliffs and get started on a hard day's work. I was there when Johnson was there, and boy, was he a rough owner. He wanted everything spick and span at all times. My father feared him and respected him, as did I. Of course, we talk about Johnson now because he disappeared on a sailboat a few years later— one of the great tragedies of my life, as I respected him so greatly. I spent years fearing the sea as a result. As a Vineyard resident, you always find new reasons to fear the sea, I suppose."

The article also mentioned Kelli and her difficulty in

selling it. Lola quoted Kelli as saying, "People don't see what I see when I bring them out there. They see a shell. They don't see what that shell represents— the colossal history beneath and what it can become once again."

Lola had also quoted Xander Van Tress, who spoke excitedly about the potential sale.

"I've never seen anything like it in my life. I want to sink my teeth into it and taste the past and the present and the future of the old place. Martha's Vineyard. Does it get any better than that?"

This was a perfect quote. Kelli's heart jumped into her throat. A crush— was that what she had? She remembered when she had first crushed on Mike. In her eyes, he could do no wrong. Hormones were a tricky thing to fight. They had no rhyme nor reason.

Kelli leaned back in her office chair and tapped her nails across the hardwood of the desk. The previous afternoon, Lexi had convinced her to get her nails done in preparation for her date with Xander. According to his text messages, he planned to pick her up at that very office in the next hour. He planned to bring her to a wine bar. What would she be like, feeling so tipsy and comfortable due to the wine with a guy she so, so wanted to kiss? Would she mess up in some way? What would she even talk about? She prayed now, to God above, that she wouldn't blather on about something boring, like the weather or what she liked to cook. What was something interesting she could talk about?

She lifted her fingers to the keyboard of her computer and typed:

INTERESTING THINGS TO BRING UP ON DATES

Oh, God. She'd really done it now. She was rusty and

uncreative. Shame washed over her as she deleted the words and scrunched her nose. Before she had a chance to consider this even more, there was a knock at the door.

"Come in!"

Brittany opened the door and grimaced. "There's a call for you."

Kelli knew it. It was Xander, wasn't it? Calling to cancel.

"It's Mike," Brittany said instead.

"Gosh. Really. What does he want?"

Men always sensed when you had moved on from them. It was their animal instincts. They had it, even from miles and miles away.

"He wouldn't say. You know how he is," Brittany informed her.

"Right." Kelli heaved a sigh and nodded. "I'll take it."

Brittany clicked the door closed and left Kelli to face the music of her phone. She took a deep breath and answered.

"Mike."

"Kelli. There she is. The woman of the hour."

Kelli's heart dropped into her belly. Mike could be charming when he wanted to be. She knew that better than anyone. Some days, they'd spent hours arguing, only for him to turn on his joking, clown face for their children, who had adored him at the time and not known the sinister backdrop of their parents' relationship.

"What do you want, Mike?"

"I want to talk about this little article I just read over," Mike stated. "About the hotel."

Mike had been involved in the dealings of the hotel before his departure. Like Kelli and her parents, he had also struggled in selling the thing.

"What about it?"

"Well, you know I never told you this, Kelli, but I always had a hunch about that old place."

"And what hunch is that?" She didn't have time for these games. Xander would be arriving soon, and she wanted to have time to do her makeup, make a mistake, wash it off, then do it again, as she always did.

"I don't actually think that place was ever legally your parents to sell," he shot then.

Kelli's heart skipped a beat at his words. "What do you mean?"

"Well, I never was able to find any proof. There is no deed. No paperwork. Nothing."

Kelli stuttered. "That's impossible. My parents always owned that property." Ever since she could remember, the issue of the property on the cliffside had been a topic of conversation. Her parents had known that they could make a killing on it yet never had found an interested buyer, especially since the property was located so far west and away from the rest of the action on the island.

Mike balked. "Yeah, you never did question your parents. That was my job, and you always resisted it because you always thought they were perfect."

"That's ridiculous. I know my parents aren't perfect. You've seen all our fights over the years."

Mike scoffed. It was impossible to convince him away from his own firmly held beliefs. Kelli knew better than to try to change his thoughts.

"In any case, there is no proof, as far as I can tell, that you should be able to sell that place. I don't know what will happen to you if you do sell it and it winds up belonging to someone else. I do know that I felt it was on my shoulders to warn you."

Kelli's nostrils flared. "Don't call here again, Mike. You left, and we're better off with you out of the picture. Do you understand me?" She then slammed the phone onto the receiver and let out a low growl.

Brittany reappeared in the doorway of her office. Her face was etched with concern. Often, when Brittany saw other people upset, she always turned into Mother Hubbard. She called herself "the ultimate empath, almost to her detriment."

"Are you okay?"

"Yes. I'll be fine after some deep breaths."

"Do you want me to go to Rhode Island and commit a crime?" Brittany asked, flashing her a mischievous grin.

Kelli laughed in spite of everything. "I don't think so, but I'll keep you posted if anything changes."

"Please do."

The moment the door clipped shut, Kelli sprung into action. The listing of the hotel was found in nearly every file her parents had passed over to her; it was on their website; it was in the paperwork they, themselves, had drawn up. But when she searched through the old deeds and older paperwork, she found nothing linked back to the old hotel.

Why did her parents think they had this to sell? Did the hotel possibly belong to someone who hadn't wanted to sell it in the first place? And why wasn't there any record of that person anywhere?

What was going on?

Kelli could feel her heart racing in her chest. If she sold a property that wasn't actually hers to sell, there would be serious consequences. Suppose that article had led someone to catch onto her "scheme"?

Suddenly, her phone buzzed with a text.

> XANDER VAN TRESS: On my way!
> Excited to see you again.

"Shoot," she muttered as she flung herself toward the bathroom. She didn't have time to go over this, but she had to pretend over the next few hours that she knew nothing about this. If this was nothing, she couldn't let Mike ruin it. Not again.

Chapter Ten

A boutique hotel called The Hesson House had recently opened its doors, with a beautiful wine bar that dripped from the immaculate yard out toward the glittering sands that stretched along the Nantucket Sound. It was here that Xander took her, here where he opened the car door of his convertible for her and helped her step delicately onto the ground below. Chivalry was still alive. His blue eyes echoed their excitement, even as he seemed still too hesitant to smile. Was it possible that Xander Van Tress was nervous at all? Probably in the city, he took women out all the time. She was just a blip on his timeline.

"What a beautiful place," Kelli breathed as she lifted her chin toward The Hesson House. "I can't believe I've never been over here."

"I spoke with the owner, Olivia Hesson," Xander continued. "I was fascinated with the fact that she built this place up to its original state— doing what I want to do so much with the Aquinnah Cliffside Overlook Hotel. I want to merge the old world with the new to bring about excitement for previous design and architecture in a new generation of tourists. She led me through the ornate dining rooms and the beautiful upstairs suites and explained the elaborate work she and her boyfriend conducted over the previous months. Apparently, her great aunt left her the mansion. The pressure of it nearly destroyed her. Ah! Look. Here she is now."

Olivia Hesson stepped down from the back porch and lifted a hand to shake Xander's. Kelli felt a funny sensation, a shiver snaking up the back of her spine. Was this jealousy? She wanted to laugh at herself. Xander had only just mentioned that Olivia had built up the property with her boyfriend. Was this proof that she liked him way more than even she could comprehend? She blushed and inwardly cursed her teenage-like mind.

"I'm so glad you came by, Xander," Olivia said brightly. "And Kelli Montgomery, right? I don't think you remember, but we were introduced many, many years ago. I believe our ex-husbands were chummy for a while."

"Ah. I see." Kelli felt the words like a punch to the stomach.

"Long ago days," Olivia affirmed with the wave of her hand. "I'll send one of the best bottles of wine over to your table. It's on the house."

"You don't have to do that," Kelli offered.

"Please, for old time's sake. Or— if not for the old times, then for the new times, as I guess they show us just how rough the old times really got."

Olivia's eyes were stern for a moment, proof, yet again, that many people on the island knew just what a waste of a human life Mike truly was.

But in a moment, the strangeness was over, and Xander placed the palm of his hand upon Kelli's back and guided her toward the table that Olivia had set aside for them. In a flash, the expensive bottle of Primitivo was sent to their table, and their glasses were filled. The sun had begun its beautiful descent toward the west and started to cast orange light upon everything. It was endlessly nostalgic, an ever-present reminder of summertime evenings Kelli could never return to. She and Xander locked eyes for a moment; perhaps this was an acknowledgment of the strangeness of first date operations. And then, they clinked glasses and took a sip.

"Wow. That is really something," Xander breathed.

Kelli knew very little about wine. She wished she would have picked Lola or Christine's brain about it prior to coming with a very rich man to a wine bar. Would that mistake cost her everything?

No, she reminded herself. What would cost her everything was the fact that the legalities of selling that Aquinnah Cliffside Overlook Hotel was suddenly iffy at best. The worst of it all was that Mike knew. He now dangled this fact above her neck; he held the ax, and she was the chicken.

"Ex-husband. That sounds complicated," Xander leaned back in his chair as he placed the napkin across his lap.

"At forty-six, everything's a bit complicated at times, I suppose," Kelli told him. "It's crazy for me to even say that's my age."

Xander chuckled. "I'm turning fifty this year. Dreading it."

"Anything big planned?"

"Maybe a sailing expedition," he answered.

"Ah. You're a sailor. No wonder you like the Vineyard."

Both of their eyes turned toward the horizon to watch as two sailboats seemed to chase after one another, making big rushing circles beneath the glow of the sunset.

"How could you not like it out there?" Xander asked softly. "I suppose you already know that I grew up poor. My father and I didn't have much. One of the first things I bought for us when I hit it big was a sailboat. Of course, neither my father nor I knew how to sail properly. Even still, we jumped out on the open waves without preparation—"

"Nothing?" Kelli was incredulous.

"I read a few books, to be honest," Xander admitted. "But those first few hours were terrifying. The winds whipped around us. I felt a fear I hadn't felt since I was quite young and my father hadn't returned from one of his odd jobs for many hours. I thought, in those moments, that I would have to find a way through my life alone."

Kelli was mesmerized at the immense information he'd just given her. She dropped her eyes toward the tablecloth. How could she be so honest with him when the one thing that had brought them together, the hotel, could be a lie in and of itself?

She was caught in a trap.

But gosh, how she wanted to feel something. How she wanted him to look at her the way he was: like she mattered, like she was the peak of his endless quest for something. She wanted that look to go on just a little bit longer before he figured everything out.

Say something, her heart urged her mind. *Say something that will make him fall for you.*

"Is there something you still do that you always did back then?" Kelli asked softly as she leaned closer to him.

"No matter how much money you have or where you are or who you are, you always return to this."

Immediately, Xander's grin widened. After a pause, he said, "Nobody has ever asked me anything like that before."

Kelli's heart pattered. She'd done something good for once in her life.

"I have an answer. It's an immediate one. Probably, there are other answers, but this is my answer to you. I still eat mac and cheese, made straight from the box. It reminds me of long-ago nights when my father decided we had enough money to pool together for a big box of the stuff."

"The yellow stuff?" Kelli laughed. "You're kidding."

"Hand on my heart. I love it. It's terrible for you, and if I ever lean too hard on it, I know these abs I've sculpted after so, so many hours in the gym will fade away."

Kelli let out a small laugh; then, a smile erupted across her mouth. Abs? Were they washboard abs? She was rather athletic herself, but even she had never seen the likes of abs, not even before her babies.

"It would be worth it, though. To drown in a big sea of mac and cheese and give up on the rest of the world," he teased. He tilted his head slightly, then asked, "But what about you?"

She tilted her head, locking eyes with him. "What do you mean?"

"I mean, tell me a secret about yourself. Something you've never told anyone."

Kelli's cheeks burned with a sudden flash of embarrassment. In her eyes, at that moment, she was the most boring creature on the planet. What had she fallen asleep watching last night? Another show on HGTV, with Lexi by her side? That's how it had gone most of the week.

"I don't know," she replied with a shrug. "I guess I'm pretty average."

"I don't believe that for a second," he told her. He took another sip and swirled the wine around his mouth. "What about if you hadn't taken over your parents' real estate business? What would you have done instead?"

"That's easy," Kelli said without pause. "And I already did it. I opened my own little vintage boutique. Clothes, furnishings, antiques, and old records, that kind of thing."

"You never mentioned you had two businesses."

Kelli loved hearing the surprise behind his voice. Was it really that impressive to operate two? Back when Mike had been around, it hadn't felt like such an undertaking. Now, Lexi had stepped up to the plate, happy to take over numerous responsibilities at the boutique.

"I miss the boutique more than I can say since I've had to switch my schedule around to accommodate the ramped-up need at the real estate office. It used to be my passion to go to old auctions and scour second-hand shops online to find the perfect designer bag from the sixties or a coat with a particular story from a previous owner. Every item I placed in the store seems taken from this other whole life, and every time I walk in, it's like I'm transported, for just a split second, to all these other worlds and realities."

As Kelli spoke, Xander's eyes widened with surprise and intrigue. "I would love to see you in your element like that," he said softly. "Hunting for these stories. Finding the beauty in what other people threw away long ago." He then chuckled again as Kelli's shoulders seemed to loosen, then fall back. "I can't believe you tried to convince me you were boring, Kelli Montgomery. You little liar."

Later, after the second glass of wine, Xander removed a folded piece of paper from his back pocket and splayed it across their table.

"I thought you'd get a kick out of this," he said. "They're the original plans I'd drawn up for the potential five-star hotel prior to actually seeing the old bones of the Aquinnah Cliffside Overlook Hotel."

Kelli peered at the fine detail and the beautiful lines but soon burst into laughter at the state of it.

"I told you." Xander looked up at her and furrowed his brows. "It's awful, isn't it?"

Kelli puffed out her cheeks. "Awful isn't the word for it."

"Foolish, then," he pushed as he folded the plans back up. "Now that I've seen old photographs of the Cliffside Overlook and dug deeper into the old-world architecture of the place, I feel like a naive architect at best. I guess it was always something of a passion of mine, architecture. But I'd never tried my hand at it before. I don't think I ever will again."

As Xander spoke, his cheeks burned red with embarrassment.

"I can't believe I even showed you," Xander ran his fingers through his hair, exhaling slowly. "I don't normally show my weaknesses like that. It goes against everything I've taught myself over the years about how to exist in society and how to impress women."

It was Kelli's turn to blush. She took a long sip of wine and returned the glass to the table. "At this stage of my life, I'm just impressed with your honesty. It's really such a rare thing to meet a man like that."

Again, she felt the punch in her gut from her lack of honesty, but the punch was lighter now, in the wake of the flowing wine.

"Thank you for coming out with me tonight," Xander said softly. He lifted a hand and placed it over hers on the white tablecloth. Toward the waterline, a violinist played a slow, nostalgic tune, which swept over the heads of the hotel guests and wine bar revelers. Kelli longed to take an emotional snapshot of this moment so that she could return to it in the days and months to come. It was a strange moment of hope and endless relief; it was a reminder that despite all the horrors of the previous years, there was still time for the story to change if only she would allow it.

Chapter Eleven

"He won't listen to reason." James paced across the hardwood of the presidential suite so much that he was going to leave a trail in his wake. His pacing was manic and his eyes alight as his thoughts performed backflips through his mind. "What I've offered him is worth far more than he might ever make in his entire lifetime. I have a hunch about his personal takeaway here as the owner."

Marilyn made an "mm-hmm" noise with her lips as they held together three bobby pins, all of them jagged and pointed toward the mirror as she styled her half-up, James-approved hairdo. Robert had told her the reason he didn't care much about money. *"The hotel is a passion project for me. I respected Johnson more than I've ever respected another man. He was more of a father than my own father. And thusly, I didn't wish for the Overlook to be anything more than an extension of his life's work. I've never craved money, never needed to be rich."* Marilyn had felt the words to be as beautiful as poetry. As she'd never had money growing up, money had been a fixation of her father's; now that she was married to James, money was a symbol of status. The ultimate aspiration of nearly everyone she and James knew was to simply make more of it.

But James spoke to her now without requiring an answer. This was a frequent situation between the two of them. He blabbered on; she allowed her thoughts to trace other pathways. Perhaps this was how marriage was supposed to work. With each passing year, you turned further and further away from one another and only acted as though it resembled a relationship.

"I can't help it, Marilyn. With every day that passes, my desire for this hotel grows. I feel wild with it. I don't suppose I will rest until my name is on the deed."

Marilyn arched an eyebrow in response. He hardly noticed. She then reached for her hairbrush and accidentally brushed aside a handkerchief in the process. Beneath it, a tiny sliver of paper appeared. She quickly lifted the handkerchief to discover that the paper was a folded note, on which someone had scribed the word "MARILYN" in beautiful handwriting.

Marilyn's heart raced in her neck like a rabbit's. She quickly placed the handkerchief over the note again to ensure her husband did not see. Luckily, he had buried himself too deep in his thoughts to notice her abrupt motions.

James dropped back on the bed they shared and splayed his hands over his eyes. He was probably hungover, as he'd spent several hours at the bar the previous night with another man from the city, who was familiar with James' father and had numerous tales from his travels across Africa. Although Marilyn was fascinated with any idea of this other world, she grew annoyed at James' frequent interruptions, as though, no matter what this man had done, James still yearned to find a way to one-up him. She had retired to her bedroom but remained wide awake for hours, her eyes following the slight crack in the ceiling as her heart had shattered with thoughts of Robert, questioning why she hadn't seen him that day or where he'd been. Did he have a love interest somewhere? Oh, but why did she demand any kind of attention from him when any time together was outside the bounds of reason— and borderline impossible?

With James on the bed in a perpetual state of feeling bad for himself, Marilyn slowly removed the folded paper and glanced within. Her body blocked any view of this from James, not that he planned to get back up any time soon.

The note read:
Meet me at the stables tomorrow at noon.
R.

There was a scream in the back of her mind. Slowly, she folded the note back up and slipped it beneath the handkerchief. She then placed her hands on her thighs and stared into space for the following five minutes, maybe ten— completely lost in the dream of whatever this was. Approximately thirty minutes later, James received a note from the man from New York, inviting him on a sailing expedition the following morning to depart at nine and arrive in the evening. How had Robert known that James would be away? Or had he somehow arranged this to happen, to steal time away with her?

It didn't matter.

James asked Marilyn if she would be able to find a way to occupy her time the following day with him gone. Marilyn nearly laughed out loud at the idea. Even without Robert's idea for their afternoon, she would have enjoyed the day alone— walking the cliffs and reading and writing in her journal. It was another sign of the horror of their dynamic that James assumed she wasn't creative enough to be alone. That or it was proof that when he was alone, he didn't have a thing to do and required constant input from outside sources.

* * *

A black beauty, the horse in the center stall, tossed her head with human-like arrogance. Marilyn, all dressed in her riding garb, giggled playfully and then splayed her hand across the horse's nose. The fur in this area was tender and smooth. The horse calmed and turned her eyes toward her.

"She likes you," Robert said. He stepped up and stretched his broad palm across the side of the horse's neck. "It's a rare thing for her to like anyone."

"I suppose I can relate," Marilyn returned.

"Should I take that as a compliment? Or is the jury still out on your feelings toward me?" Robert asked. He turned so that his eyes caught hers there in the dark shadows of the stables. A ball of anxiety quivered in the base of Marilyn's stomach. Was this lust? Or fear? Or a combination of both, a storm apt to drive her wild?

It had been absolutely nothing to leave her room and meet Robert. The real trouble had come in the night when she had again struggled to sleep due to the intensity of her emotions. A storm billowed across her head and her heart. This was not the first time she imagined what it would be like to leave James forever. It was an impossibility, just a dream. Perhaps she would dream it forever.

Marilyn was suddenly quiet. She watched as Robert saddled the horse and then saddled his own. His motions were quick and precise; his muscles flickered beneath the fabric of his riding shirt. Her fingers itched to feel the strength. When he flashed his eyes back toward her, he said, "You know, I don't think I've seen this horse take to anyone except Mr. Johnson prior to you."

Mr. Johnson. Again, everything seemed linked to this man, who had apparently disappeared out at sea. Sorrow was etched across Robert's face when he spoke of him. But she knew this from a long-ago era when her sister had died at age three. The only way to keep the memory of her alive was to speak of her. Robert knew this, as well.

They rode side-by-side. Marilyn often went riding with James, times that had always resulted in his riding up ahead of her, striding forth, as though he wanted to prove himself the faster, braver rider. This was far different.

After nearly a mile of riding near the cliff's edge, Robert ducked them inward and sped his horse up. Marilyn took this as a sudden challenge. She tapped her heels into the belly of her black beauty and then sped up to match him. He wholeheartedly laughed, tossing his head back so that his locks flew with the wind.

"You're certainly no city girl, are you, Marilyn?"

Marilyn was so grateful that he didn't use her husband's last name. She felt no allegiance to the name Peterson.

"Indeed, you are correct. You can take a girl out of the country, but you can't take the country out of the girl." She then dug her heels in tighter and picked up speed as Robert's laughter chased after her.

An hour later, they reached the northern edge of the island, only a half-mile from the center of Oak Bluffs.

"This is my neck of the woods," Robert explained. "I now live in a little room at the hotel, but just to keep an eye on things during the busier months. When it slows down, I stay over here in town. I help my parents with odd jobs, see my sisters, and drink with friends. I then pretend that I didn't take on one of the biggest responsibilities of my life in taking over this hotel after Mr. Johnson."

He stopped his horse and slipped off. He rushed around to assist Marilyn with her disembarking, but she popped off without assistance. He whistled, then took the reins of her horse and tied them to a nearby fence. They then took their time walking across the sand, their fingers very nearly brushing as they went.

"Do you regret it, then?" Marilyn asked. She dared not to look in his eyes; she felt that his gaze was as bright as the sun. "Taking the hotel, I mean."

"That's a difficult question," Robert breathed. "Because I adored Mr. Johnson and I would have said yes to anything he'd asked. But now, I hardly sleep. I worry endlessly about the hotel. I pray that I'm keeping it up in all the ways Mr. Johnson would have appreciated." His smile was crooked then as he added, "I hope you won't tell your husband about my hesitations around the place. I wouldn't dream of selling it to him."

"Even if it would take the stress of it off your shoulders forever?"

He shook his head. "That's not to say it isn't alluring. I just simply couldn't bring myself to do it."

"You have integrity, Robert Sheridan," Marilyn whispered. "That's a rare thing in this world."

"I'd like to carry it forward, even as so many forget it altogether," Robert returned softly.

They caught one another's gaze as a wind dragged a wave forth to crash along the beach, mere feet from where they stood. Marilyn was captivated. It was as though the crash of the waves shook through her belly, through her very soul, and pointed out a very strange truth: she wasn't sure she'd ever fallen in love before. Was this what it felt like— all this anxiety and worry, stirring against waves of passion?

Robert lifted a hand. Marilyn's eyes closed as his fingers fluttered across her cheek. He collected a strand of hair and pressed it gently behind her ear.

"You wear your hair differently when you're not with him," he said then.

Marilyn kept her eyes closed. In the darkness, her other senses were hyper-focused. The salty sea air, the musk of Robert's skin, the coming autumn— it all stirred through her nose as the sound of the waves roared through the air. She could even hear the thumping of her heart within her ribcage, threatening to break free.

"I wonder if I could kiss you," Robert murmured then. He said it as though he spoke about the weather or some other commonplace thing.

"Oh." Marilyn's cheeks burned with embarrassment. When was the last time James had kissed her? He reached for her in the night, but that was often not for kissing— just for the immediacy of what he needed, which had nothing to do with romance.

Robert bridged the distance between them, but still, he didn't kiss her. Perhaps he felt it was rude.

"Do you think if I sold him the hotel, that would be enough to satisfy his happiness? To the point that if I were to whisk you away, he wouldn't notice you left him?"

Marilyn blinked somberly. "I don't know."

Was it too forward what he had said? She wasn't sure. But also, it didn't bother her, not really. It was fast, but in every way, it felt true and much bigger than anything else she'd ever experienced.

Robert stepped back again. There was hope behind his gaze. It was silly to hope for anything, especially given her parents' arrangement with James and his family. There was so much Robert couldn't understand.

But when they reached the horses once more, Robert committed it: the heinous act that swept Marilyn off her feet and stopped her heart and made the world stop turning on its axis for just a moment. He kissed her with wild and unencumbered passion. And in the space of that kiss, Marilyn felt she could see their future stretched out before them, as bright and sure as the sunshine above.

Chapter Twelve

"There he is. Mark Van Tress. I guess I'll be seeing much, much more of you over the next few years, huh?" Wes Sheridan greeted the older man at Kelli's parents' place the following afternoon. He placed a beer in his hand as Trevor entered the house from the back porch, where smoke billowed up from the grill.

"We heard a little rumor you took a liking to the old Cliffside Property," Trevor affirmed.

Mark's smile was youthful, despite his seventy-five years. He removed the top from his beer and lifted it, gesturing toward Kelli, who remained in the corner, her thoughts racing. She hadn't known her father had invited the Van Tresses for his barbecue that evening; in fact, she'd wanted to take the opportunity of the dinner party to sit aside with her parents and dig a bit deeper into their memories regarding the old Cliffside Overlook. If it potentially wasn't theirs to sell, then why had they made a big fuss over it all these years? And why then, if those blueprints actually belonged to the Cliffside Overlook, had they been in her parents' attic all this time?

"She's been a tremendous help," Mark said as he beamed at Kelli. "I've met countless real estate agents on Xander and I's quest to find our luxury hotel properties. Your daughter here is perhaps the best I've ever worked with."

Trevor beamed at Kelli. "We think she's pretty amazing ourselves, even though we may be just a tad biased."

"That's putting it lightly." This was Lola, who rushed in from the kitchen, rubbing her wet hands over a towel. She flashed a smile and then said, "That article got a huge number of readers. My editor was very pleased. He wants me to put together a book over the next few years about important historical sights on Martha's Vineyard, if you can believe it, inspired by this article."

"Oh! You should do exclusively old ghost stories."

Charlotte stepped in from the kitchen with this suggestion as Rachel hustled up beside her and screeched, "No! Not ghost stories, Mom."

"Why? You scared?" Charlotte asked, giving her daughter a sideways glance.

Rachel wrinkled her nose. "Ghost stories are lame." She said it half-heartedly, as though she couldn't fully believe it.

"That's not what she thought last week when we told them around the campfire," her cousin, Gail, said as she jumped in from the porch. "You told Abby she had to stop."

Rachel glowered at Gail and mouthed, "Gee, thanks."

Kelli chuckled inwardly, despite all her swirling fears.

Lexi followed in from the porch after Gail, her hand filled with chips. Kelli beckoned for her, and Lexi begrudgingly handed her mother several chips. Each slice was a perfect balance of oil and salt on Kelli's tongue.

"You know, you can really go out and get your own chips, Mom," Lexi teased.

"Oh, you hush," Kelli returned. She wiped her hands lightly on the top of her pants and then said, "How did it go at the boutique today?"

"I had a huge sale today, actually," Lexi announced. "That old vintage coat— the cream one from Paris in the 1960s..."

"You sold it?" Kelli was amazed. The coat had hung with its incredible six hundred dollar price tag for the previous nine months. She hadn't imagined anyone would purchase it at that price, especially not in the height of summer.

"I don't know what came over this woman, but she nearly crumpled when she spotted it on the rack," Lexi explained with excitement. "I played it cool, of course, even though on the inside I really wanted to scream, *buy that coat!*"

"Wow. Six hundred dollars in a single sale. That's a rare thing." Kelli whistled as her stomach settled the slightest bit. Her second thought was that she couldn't wait to tell Mike, as he always belittled the concept of the boutique and thought it was a money-waster. Then, she remembered she no longer had to tell him anything.

Xander hadn't yet arrived by the time Kerry demanded everyone sit around the large table out near the water. The menu was barbecue chicken and fresh fruit and peppers, blackened in spots by the grill. Mark left a space beside him at the table and said to Trevor, "Xander should be here shortly. He had a few phone calls to make regarding other properties."

"Sounds like you and your son are trying to take over the world," Kerry shot out. This was the tone of voice Kelli found most difficult to read when Kerry used it; here, Kelli was pretty sure Kerry insinuated that the men were rather greedy, that they shouldn't have taken up so much space on earth. Still, these sorts of men were the real estate company's bread and butter— and Kerry knew that.

"We have a good time scavenging around the earth, finding these properties," Mark agreed without skipping a beat. Yet again, Kerry's subtle tone had slipped through the conversation without detection.

"And Kelli, I heard that you and Xander met at The Hesson House just last night," Kerry said then. Her eyes bore into Kelli's as she announced this across the table. "Was this to go over the contract? It's a beautiful but strange location for such a thing. We must go there together soon. It's been the talk of the island."

It felt as though several stones fell into the base of Kelli's stomach. She swallowed the lump in her throat as Mark lifted an eyebrow in confusion. Why had she thought she and Xander could go just anywhere on their date? Martha's Vineyard was a teeny little place; everyone knew everyone else. Probably, she and Xander had been at The Hesson House for no more than five minutes before Kerry had received fifteen text messages and seven phone calls.

"You and Xander met yesterday?" Mark asked. "He didn't mention it."

Kelli gave her mother an annoyed smile, which Kerry matched in return. Maybe Kerry didn't approve of the match? Maybe she thought Kelli now played with fire as she attempted to "date" a man who very well could take this property off their hands, once and for all? It was to be an enormous sale, the likes of which would stabilize the real estate company in the coming years. Kerry was a diligent businesswoman. Still, she didn't know what it was like out there for single women. It wasn't easy, that was for sure. And what was Kelli supposed to do in the face of this gorgeous man? Ignore his advances?

"Ah. Speak of the devil," Mark said.

Kelli nearly leaped from her skin as she turned to watch Xander stride across the yard. Only just last night, he had dropped her off in front of her house, turned off the engine, and actually walked her to the door. Kelli shoved away thoughts of Mike then. He had never been the sort of guy to walk a woman to the door. Even after only a few months of marriage, he'd hardly bothered to help her bring the groceries from the car to the kitchen.

"Hello, everyone," Xander greeted with a wide grin. He paused at the head of the table, his mouth slightly crooked. "I apologize for being late."

"It's no problem. Don't worry yourself," Kerry told him brightly. She jumped to her feet with much more youth and vitality than her seventy-two years should have allowed, then promptly gestured toward a chair far from where Kelli now sat, as though she'd set it there on purpose to keep the two of them away from one another.

Kelli felt like a teenager. She remembered long-ago days when her mother had watched her like a hawk. There had never been enough honesty between them back then for the sort of conversations Kelli herself had had with her daughter about teenage drinking and safe sex. During that time, parents had known only to speak the language of fear. Kelli couldn't blame her mother for that, of course. It was just the way things had been back then.

"This is delicious, Mrs. Montgomery," Xander complimented a few minutes later. His voice boomed over the others' as his eyes found Kerry's over the table. He had a fork lifted; it glistened with barbecue sauce. "I have to admit, I've never been as well-fed as I have been since Dad and I arrived on the island."

"It's just our way, Mr. Van Tress," Kerry said. She layered on the syrup, knowing full well this was how you treated a client mid-way toward a sale. You had to treat them like no one else mattered in the world. "We're so happy to welcome you and hope you plan to spend a good deal of time on our beautiful island."

"The winter months scare me," Mark interjected.

"Oh, Mark, didn't you spend a few weeks with us during a winter back in the seventies?" Wes tried as he furrowed his brow.

"And that is precisely why I'm frightened," Mark replied, chuckling. "I remember the wind howling so loudly every night that I couldn't fall asleep. When I awoke, two feet of snow had piled itself up against the door. You and I spent the whole day and night drinking whiskey and heating up cans of soup."

"Dad, wow," Lola remarked with wide eyes. "That's quite an image."

"Your mother was right along with us," Wes said with a mischievous grin.

"That's right. She outdrank me, for certain." Mark wagged his knife through the air. "That Anna was a spitfire."

Kelli made a mistake then of glancing Xander's way.

A Vineyard Rebirth

The table had grown quiet in the wake of the mention of Anna, one of their ghosts. Xander bowed his head slightly but kept his eyes upon hers. There was acceptance behind his irises, acceptance of the many messes of the Montgomery and Sheridan family and knowledge that he, too, brought his own share of previous trauma. Kelli broke eye contact a moment later, flashing her eyes back toward Lexi so that she could drum up a conversation about the boutique and the plans for the new design in the shop window.

As the night wore on, Kerry made multiple efforts to keep Xander and Kelli apart. Kelli could have laughed aloud at some of the obstacles she created— even demanding that she show Xander all the little flowers she'd begun to grow on the south edge of the house and asking Wes and Trevor to take Xander on a walk along the water while she and Kelli and Lola cleaned dishes in the kitchen. As Kelli scrubbed a particularly heinous sauce stain from a plate, Lola watched the men out the window and whistled.

"He really is a handsome man, isn't he?"

Kerry arched an eyebrow. "I don't know about that."

"I know, Aunt Kerry. You only have eyes for Uncle Trevor," Lola teased. "But the rest of us aren't married yet."

"Ah, but what about your handsome sailor?" Kerry demanded.

Lola chuckled. "Tommy and I are doing very, very well, Aunt K. Very well. Admittedly, it's difficult to get him to come home from his sailing expeditions, especially during the summertime. But I spend more time at the Sheridan house when he's gone, which suits me just fine. I have a new grandbaby, you know."

Kerry traced her gaze across Lola's face, down her shoulders. "You? A grandmother? It seems outside the realms of science." She then turned her gaze toward Kelli and asked, "When do you think you'll become a grandmother, then? Sam's getting up there in years."

"Sam's twenty-one," Kelli pointed out. "And he can do exactly as he pleases for as long as he wants." She hoped her mother saw what she really meant: that, in fact, she planned to do exactly as she wanted to, for as long as she wanted to. If she could manage it, that is. "Besides. All the kids have had a hard time since, well, since their father left."

This shut everyone up for a long time. There was just the sizzle of the radio speakers and the rush of the faucet water. Night had begun to move over them. Shadows moved across the yard and curved beneath the house. Very soon, Lexi appeared to say that she needed to get back, as she wanted to be at the boutique around seven the following morning to do inventory.

"She's turning into a little businesswoman!" Kerry cried as she wrapped her arms around her granddaughter and beamed.

"She really is," Kelli affirmed.

Xander appeared in the doorway and gave her a firm nod. He recognized the distance between them and seemed to comprehend that he couldn't get closer to her, not under the watchful eyes of Kerry Montgomery.

Everyone called out their goodnights as Kelli and Lexi headed out. Kelli's legs felt loose and unreliable beneath her. When she collapsed in the front seat of her car, her phone buzzed with a text message from Xander.

XANDER: I'd love to take you sailing.

> XANDER: Just us.
>
> XANDER: But only if you're up for it.
>
> XANDER: P.S. (and here lies words in a business context) I am looking forward to signing the papers and officially purchasing that gorgeous property. Let me know when we can set up an official meeting. But I hope I can take you out on the water first.

"What are you smiling about?" Lexi clicked her seatbelt together and blinked at her mother incredulously.

"Oh, nothing."

"Right. I totally believe you." Lexi rolled her eyes playfully.

"What's gotten into you?" Kelli asked.

"Oh. Nothing," Lexi mimicked.

Kelli started the engine. For a long time as she drove home, she thought only of the softness of Xander's hand on her lower back and of the certainty behind his eyes as he gazed at her across the table. He already seemed to fit into the rest of her family, as though he had been a missing puzzle piece all this time.

Still, her mother was correct. If something shifted between them prior to making the official sale, then the sale would be lost. But her mother and Xander didn't know the potential that Mike had yanked to the surface—that, in fact, the hotel wasn't theirs to sell. Kelli's stomach quaked with anxiety. It would be a long, sleepless night.

Chapter Thirteen

The July sunlight was an impossibly delicious sight. It stirred with the wind and draped itself lovingly over Kelli's skin. She arched her back and lifted her chin toward the horizon line as she maintained her balance— legs bird-like and spread apart as the sailboat quaked beneath her and the waves flirted against the base.

"Are you ever going to open your eyes?" Xander laughed from several feet away.

Kelli felt as though she awoke from a dream. Her eyelashes fluttered open, and she found him, sun-drenched and tanned, one of the ropes flung through his confident hands.

Kelli wore nothing except a black bikini. She'd stood in front of her floor-to-ceiling mirror that morning in only that, inspecting every inch of her forty-six-year-old body. Ultimately, she had decided to say, "What the heck?" and packed it away for this very occasion. If Xander didn't appreciate the subtle stretch marks from her having carried three babies; if he didn't appreciate the way time had worked its way across her form yet still left it intact, incredibly capable— then perhaps he wasn't worth her time, anyway.

"You look absolutely beautiful, Kelli Montgomery," Xander complimented as his hair flew wildly in the wind.

And in fact, she felt beautiful. It was a rare thing that a man could draw out this feeling within her. It felt like a flower unfurling itself in her stomach. She stepped toward him and positioned her hands on his shoulders, where the muscles cascaded beautifully from the top and down his back.

"You're like a sculpture," she beamed.

"I suppose I'm just as cold and stoic as a sculpture, too."

"No, not at all." Kelli paused and furrowed her brow. They still hadn't kissed. Was this the moment? But then, a larger wave rollicked against the side of the boat and pushed them to and fro. Kelli had to drop a foot back behind her and follow the tilt of the boat to keep herself from falling.

"Your mother is really something," Xander stated a few minutes later. The sails above rippled and filled with the wind, and their speed escalated.

Kelli perched at the edge of the boat and busied herself with the top of a bottle of champagne, which she had brought for the special afternoon, like some sort of teenager with an urgent desire to celebrate.

"She knows everything and everyone," Kelli admitted. "She's always terrified me."

"She cares for everyone in that family to an incredible degree, doesn't she?" Xander asked.

"She picked up a lot of slack after Aunt Anna died," Kelli explained. Finally, she tugged off the champagne cork; bubbles shot to the surface and then receded before tumbling out. Xander whistled, clearly impressed, as she dropped the bottle over her lips and drank straight. Her head fizzed.

"And then last year, when Wes got really sick and nearly burned down the house, my mother was instrumental in bringing back the Sheridan girls," Kelli continued. "She grumbled about it a lot before she finally called Susan. She said she wasn't sure the girls deserved to have their family back since they had abandoned the island all those years ago. But ultimately, these were just words. Not what she actually felt. She genuinely believes in second chances. She genuinely believes in keeping families together. Well, until my husband, I suppose." She took another sip from the champagne bottle as Xander studied her.

After a long pause, he said, "I appreciate you being so open with me."

Kelli dropped her chin. "I don't know if I really am being so open."

Xander shrugged. "Feels like I've been out with so many women at this point. Women who only talk about commonplace things. Women who say things about the weather."

"I can talk all day about the weather," Kelli teased. "What do you want to know about it? Today it's sunny, maybe eight-three degrees. Wind out of the east."

"I think it's actually out of the west," Xander said with a wink.

Kelli laughed as she dropped her head back. "My mother would kill me if she knew I was out here with you. And I somehow like that feeling. It reminds me of being a kid again. I miss getting into trouble. How boring it is to be an adult. Always paying your bills on time. Always saying and doing the right thing."

Xander stood again and slowly walked toward her. His blue eyes caught the light wonderfully; they seemed to reflect back the immensity of the ocean around them.

"You have freckles today," he told her. "I've never noticed them before."

"They used to always come out beneath the sun," she said. "But I guess I haven't spent so much time in the sun lately."

"You look beautiful," he told her softly.

He then splayed a hand across her cheek as she closed her eyes; her knees locked, then unlocked, as his soft, pillow-like lips fell over hers. Her heart pulsed and then quickened. They floated there, in the impossibility of this moment, beneath the July sunlight and over the fury of the ocean. Nothing seemed real— not this kiss, nor her emotions, nor the bright rock just to the left of them, the island on which she'd been born and where she knew, one day, she would die.

* * *

Kelli returned to her house around five-thirty. Lexi remained at the boutique until six. Kelli decided to change clothes and head to the real estate office to discuss various properties with her other employees, check on the status of everyone's sales, and investigate further into the issue of the Cliffside Overlook. Perhaps she had overlooked a paper. She hadn't heard from Mike since his threatening phone call. He'd probably made the whole thing up to poison her mind and mess with her. That was a very Mike-like thing to do.

On her drive back to the real estate office, she received a call from Brittany.

"Hey girl!" she called into the speaker system as she continued her route. "I'm headed your way."

"Oh. Gosh, good," Brittany returned. Her voice sounded panicked. "There's someone here to speak with you."

Kelli's heart quickened. "Oh?"

"Just get here as fast as you can, okay?"

Kelli parked her car and rushed for the door, grateful she'd donned a summer dress with a business jacket and a pair of heels. She'd had half a mind to keep her beach garb on, just a little flowered dress and a pair of sandals.

Brittany removed the phone from her ear as Kelli entered and mouthed, "He's in your office."

Kelli furrowed her brow. "Mike? Tell me it's not Mike?"

Brittany shook her head. Kelli's heart slowed the slightest bit. At least it wasn't him.

The man who awaited her on the other side of her desk was a stranger. He was formidable, a clear lawyer-type with a Type-A haircut and an overly-shiny face, as though he couldn't manage to grow a proper beard. He stood and lifted a hand, which Kelli shook.

"Good afternoon, Ms. Montgomery. My name is Jackson Reynolds."

"Good afternoon." Kelli shifted the door closed. She felt utterly exposed. "Can I help you?"

Mr. Reynolds placed a file folder on her desk and then opened it with a flick of his hand. The papers within were clear copies of an old deed. Kelli clicked her heels toward the desk and peered down.

It appeared to be the old deed for none other than the Aquinnah Cliffside Overlook Hotel.

Her lips formed a round O in surprise.

Her eyes flickered up toward Jackson Reynolds. "Did Mike send you?"

Jackson Reynolds shook his head, disgruntled. "I don't know anyone named Mike." He said the word "Mike" as though it was the lowest form of a name. "I'm a representative of the James Peterson Estate. It's come to our attention that you have been attempting to sell the property on the Cliffside, which has belonged to James Peterson since 1943, as you can see here." He flashed a finger toward the bottom of the page, where James Peterson, whoever that was, had signed his name and the date: September 17, 1943.

"Huh." Kelli was incredulous. She lifted the page higher. She wasn't entirely certain, but she was pretty sure that the hurricane that had destroyed the hotel had occurred sometime around September. "Bad timing?"

"If you proceed with this sale, you will find yourself up to your ears in legal consequences," he told her then. "Good afternoon, Ms. Montgomery. My information is located on a card within the folder."

He then headed toward the door and exited without another word. Kelli's stomach felt soured. Sweat billowed up across her neck and along her forehead. James Peterson. Who on earth is that?

She took to the internet first. She typed his name into the search engine. Unfortunately, James Peterson was a pretty common name, with hundreds of results. The search: "James Peterson Martha's Vineyard" came up dry, as well.

As if on cue, her phone rang again. This time, it was

the antiquarian Frederick Bachman who announced that he had finally been able to stabilize the blueprints. "They're all flattened out and much easier to read," he explained in a dry tone. "Perhaps you'd like to come by and pick them up?"

"Yes. I would love that," she told him. "I'll be there in the next half-hour."

It had been an incredibly emotional day. Kelli's eyes filled with tears as she drove to the man's tiny cottage, filled with his collection of treasures. When she parked in his driveway, she dry-heaved for nearly fifteen seconds before her brain found a way to calm itself down. She swiped at her cheeks and around her eyes, then muttered, "Pull yourself together," at the mirror. It would have to be enough.

"Mr. Bachman," she said as he eased open the door slowly. It creaked bit-by-bit as he revealed just a sliver of the outside light to his inner dungeon. "So good to see you again."

Kelli would have bet a lot of money that the man hadn't seen the outside world since she'd last seen him. How much of that time had he spent poring over the blueprints? Did he ever make time to sleep?

"This has been a very exciting project for me," Frederick told her as they hovered over the blueprints. "As you know, the document was incredibly damaged over the years, but with a few tricks of the old trade, I managed to bring it to life again. Rumor has it that the old Cliffside Hotel might be built back to its former glory. Goodness me, if I had a hand in making that happen... I would be thrilled."

Again, Kelli's eyes glazed over. She gazed at the

glorious blueprints, merging this architectural calculation with the photographs she'd seen from the twenties.

"It must have been like a fantasy," she whispered.

"No. The fantasy is now," Frederick corrected her. He flicked the side of his head playfully. "For now, the place only exists in our minds— and therefore, it's far more beautiful than any place in the world because we get to give it the magic it needs."

"But wouldn't it be incredible if we could share in that magic together?" Kelli asked.

Frederick, who was forever a loner, couldn't quite comprehend this. He gave a slight shrug and stepped away as she continued to study the document. She then reached for the folder that the lawyer had brought her and lifted the old deed toward Frederick.

"I've just learned that the hotel belongs to someone I've never heard of. I'd always been told it ran in my family," she said, her eyes still trained on the blueprints in front of her.

Frederick's eyes twinkled. "A secret."

"I suppose so," she admitted. "Although it seems to make everything much more complicated."

Frederick chuckled. "Why don't you go down to the library? There are many books about the old hotel written prior to its collapse. Photographs that the internet has never seen. Maybe you could uncover something. Who knows?" He tapped his nose playfully. "Isn't it a strange thing that humans are the only animals on earth who claim to own property? I've always been amazed by this. None of us really own anything. Our lives are so finite. Maybe things and property own us, instead."

Chapter Fourteen

September 16th

Marilyn scribed the date at the top of her diary and then blinked up to catch the last rays of the glistening autumn sun as it bobbed at the top of the cliff. She whispered goodnight to another day on Martha's Vineyard, and her heart dripped with panic at the loss of time. James had told her point-blank that if Robert continued to retreat from his advances regarding the hotel, they would return to the city within the week.

Since that first horseback ride outing, Robert had managed to steal Marilyn away five additional times. James was quite easy to convince to do anything; Robert had simply to insinuate that the particular event or get-together was something high-caliber, for only high-rollers upon the island. Each night, Marilyn watched as James prepared himself for the evening ahead, donning a tuxedo and running a comb through his hair as he informed Marilyn, yet again, that these sorts of events weren't appropriate for women. Marilyn feigned interest until the moment James clipped the door closed. Then, she flung herself into action, dropping her hair into loose curls and donning a dress. Often over the past week, Robert had had something set aside especially for her so that they could dine in his room alone and gaze into one another's eyes.

They'd taken things too far already. Marilyn had never thought of herself as dishonest, yet here she was, acting out the dramatic part of a cheating wife. Robert had made it very clear already that he would do anything to be with her, to keep her on the island with him. But James was the competitive sort. No, he didn't love her, not really— but he would never give her up. Not even for this hotel. She knew that.

September 16, 1943

I don't quite know what to make of all of this. I feel caught in the center of a storm. The winds whip around me and pull me deeper into these tumultuous, dark, yet impossibly beautiful clouds of emotion. The idea of returning to our life in New York City, where I'm only a ghost in the midst of the rest of James's life, fills me with a sense of loss and horror I can't fully explain. It's as though I'm pregnant with the idea of something— and I'll have to kill the idea, eventually, in order to survive.

Robert won't sell the hotel. It's latched to his heart, a symbol of his respect for Mr. Johnson and all they went through together. But James won't remain on the island without the hotel in his grasp. Oh, men and their sinister egos. Oh, how many wars have been fought in the name of just this? In fact, we fight one now— we're entrenched in

Germany, waging war with a madman, while I remain here with my own madman, a man so rich he managed to con his way out of the service. In Robert's case, he longed to go, to fight alongside his countrymen, but there's something off with his leg. I notice it sometimes. A slight limp. Apparently, he had an accident when he was a teenager. He calls them his "reckless" years. How I long to sift through the pages of his mind and read those stories.

Suddenly, James bolted through the door. Marilyn snapped her diary closed and spun round to catch him. His eyes were frantic, his hair a wild cloud around his head. He muttered to himself as his hands shifted over his pockets. Often, he would get drunk too early before dinner, and his empty stomach made him hyperactive and boyish.

"James. Are you all right?" She felt like a doting mother.

"Just fine. Just fine." He sniffed as he dropped down on the side of the bed. "I've planned to meet Jefferson again this evening in Oak Bluffs. He has a business proposition—a potential doozy. I've told him I still have the intention to buy this place — and he laughed in my face and told me to tag along with him instead. 'Old Robert is too sentimental to sell the place,' he snapped. I suppose that's what this island operates on. Nostalgia. Belief in their own bullshit. I believe in nothing more than profit and revenue, and I believe that makes me smarter than most men in America."

Marilyn cooed even as her heart darkened. If she agreed with him, he would leave sooner. Then, she could slip down the stairs and weave her way to Robert's bedroom, where she would inform him of James's dividing line: if he wouldn't sell, he would leave with

Marilyn in tow. Perhaps they would never see one another again. The island would represent a failure in James's life. And James never liked to look twice at his failures.

* * *

Robert's bedroom was utilitarian. It had a single bed, a gray comforter, and a single lamp. When he called for her to enter, she found him seated at the edge of the bed with his neck bent down and his hands clasped together. Her heart jumped into her throat.

"Are you all right, Robert?" She hurried into the room, gently closing the door behind her. She had the sudden urge to leap upon him and throw her arms around him. She held herself back as his eyes shifted upward.

There was silence for a long time. It ballooned between them and became so powerful. Marilyn's ears rang.

"I saw you and James together at lunch," Robert breathed. "And I remembered the other night. How strange I felt, as though I'd known you my entire life. Then to see you there with your glass of wine and your conversation and the way you could act with him, as though you'd never been with me at all..."

Marilyn again thought of the bullish nature of male egos. But she also had felt something similar, something akin to jealousy, when she'd seen Robert in conversation with one of the other female guests. She'd made him laugh, and the laughter had rocketed off the walls and crept into Marilyn's brain. Her brain had caught fire.

"I don't want to lose you," Marilyn whispered.

Robert shook his head delicately. "I don't want to lose you, either."

"James has told me that he will leave soon if you won't sell," Marilyn explained, taking a step closer.

Robert dropped his chin. "And I suppose you would go with him."

"I have to," Marilyn returned. "I can't disappoint my family. I have to ensure they're all right. This marriage has given them endless comfort. It's allowed them to breathe again."

"But what about your breath? What about your time? What about your life?"

Marilyn gave a lackluster shake of her shoulder. Robert stepped up from his bed. He looked volatile and brash, as though he might have punched anyone who stepped in his path. He didn't look like a man who owned the luxury hotel in which they now stood.

"If the world were different, I would fall in love with you, unencumbered," Marilyn told him, surprising herself with her honesty. "If only the world were different."

Robert's smile was almost sinister in its sorrow. "Why do you think it can't be different?"

"You know things don't change so quickly. Even after any war, we fight hard to try to make things go back to the way they used to be. Maybe a small part of me also understands that. Maybe a small part of me wants to cling to all I've ever known."

"Then that small part of you wants to die in misery," Robert blared.

Marilyn's eyes glistened. "That's a horrible thing to say." Her heart pounded. He glared at her severely. Perhaps this was his animal instinct, wanting to destroy her before she could rip into him.

She lurched around, gripped the door handle, and swept herself into the hallway. She'd never truly fought with someone before, not like this, not with this much passion bubbling beneath the surface. She'd normally just let James get whatever he wanted, as it was easier that way—like interacting with a toddler.

"Marilyn. Wait—" Robert cried as she fled.

But it was too late. Marilyn ran up the steps and rushed into the presidential suite, where she collapsed onto the sheets and cried. Outside, a strong wind pressed itself against the gorgeous old building making the wood and stones creak. The sound felt like some kind of warning. Marilyn lifted her eyes toward the window and marveled at the anger of the wide world around them, as though summer had been a farce before the real drama of autumn.

"Is that you, God?" she whispered. "If it is you, I hope you hear me. I hope you know what pain I'm in. And I hope you show me a way through all of this. Whatever that route may be."

Chapter Fifteen

When Kelli reached the library, she discovered that a number of historic Martha's Vineyard books had already been checked out. She smacked her fist on her thigh and ogled the gap in the shelf. Who on this earth had such a burning desire to discover the inner mechanisms of Martha's Vineyard in the previous century?

Still, she had a funny hunch that all luck wasn't lost. She rushed from the library and made her way down the little stone staircase as she hunted for the appropriate cell phone number. By the time she reached her car again, a familiar voice had sprung up on the line.

"Kelli! So good to hear from you. What can I do for you?"

"Lola. I wonder if you might be able to help me with something. It's kind of an emergency."

"Of course! Anything for my beautiful cousin."

Sure enough, Lola had the books. She'd set them all aside on a large wooden desk in the house she shared with Tommy Gasbarro. They were piled high, monstrous in their density, and Lola clucked her tongue from a few feet back and said, "Yep. It's a huge undertaking, and I am just not sure how to attack it. I told you my editor wants a fun little book about the historical life of Martha's Vineyard. But there's nothing fun about giving your entire life away to reading."

"I don't know about that," Kelli teased.

Lola hurried to the kitchen and brewed them each a cup of tea. As the water boiled, she rubbed her eyes and complained of fatigue. "You probably didn't see that Max is here sleeping over there in his crib. But it means I didn't get so much sleep last night. I wanted to give Audrey a break, and I think she's slept the previous twenty hours, maybe more. But I've been lonely since Tommy left again a few days ago, and I haven't heard from him. He's probably halfway across the Atlantic by now."

Baby Max stirred slightly in his crib. Kelli's heart cracked at the sight of this soft, innocent form, so tender and apart from all the inner chaos of her own mind.

"Really? Tommy would go all the way across the ocean?"

Lola shrugged. "That wasn't his plan. But he's kind of a free spirit. It appeals to me— and it's the reason I fell head over heels for him. But I can't help but worry—I kind of hate this about myself. I'll be forty in August. I'm a grandmother. I wonder if I've just lost my edge."

"Lola Sheridan could never lose her edge," Kelli assured her.

"I hope you're right, Kelli. In the meantime, I hope you don't mind Max is here. He's somehow soothing to me, and it makes me happy to know that Audrey can think about other things. Like her career, her budding relationship, and about the fact that she's twenty years old and on the brink of everything."

"On the brink of everything." Kelli swallowed and then turned her eyes to the ground. "That's strangely how I've felt the past few weeks. It's a feeling I thought I'd never feel again. Not at forty-six, anyway."

Lola set her jaw as she placed the mug of tea upon the old desk. "Tell me everything you can."

Kelli explained what she could about her current situation, down to the fact that she wasn't entirely sure what to do about the old hotel, as she didn't want anything to affect her budding romance with Xander Van Tress.

"I feel so dishonest in showing him the place," she whispered. "And I have no idea who this James Peterson even is or was. I don't know. My next stop is to talk to my parents about it, of course, but in the meantime, I thought I'd do some research here. Apparently, with you by my side. I feel so lucky about that."

Lola cracked her knuckles. "This is exactly the kind of work I'm up for today. Hard research. James Peterson and the Mystery of the Aquinnah Cliffside Overlook Hotel. On it."

The book pile seemed to cover every given genre in relation to Martha's Vineyard.

A History of Whaling on Martha's Vineyard
The Deaf Colonies of Martha's Vineyard
The Rise of Tourism on Martha's Vineyard
African American History on Martha's Vineyard
Wildlife of Martha's Vineyard

The collection went on and on.

"What did the librarian say when you checked out all of these books?" Kelli asked with a vibrant laugh.

Lola buzzed her lips. "I went to high school with her,

so she just asked if I was still up to my old tricks, and I said yes, and she laughed and let me take all of them. She did say that she would bill me if they were late."

"And when are they due?"

"Who knows. Probably like last week," Lola returned, rolling her eyes. "I don't know about you, but I always feel like time operates with its own rules in the summertime. Hard to believe I've been back on the Vineyard for a whole year. But harder still to believe I was away for so, so long."

They got to work: Kelli poring through one book while Lola scattered herself through several, which she said was a more appropriate way for her brain to operate. Occasionally, Lola popped up to check on baby Max while Kelli continued to read, her forehead wrinkles deepening with each passing hour.

"There's so much information about the Cliffside Overlook when Johnson was the owner," Kelli finally said, exasperated. "But nothing after that. He disappeared out to sea a few years before the hurricane. Then, in 1943, the hotel was signed over to James Peterson. But I can't find record of him anywhere."

"Hmm." Lola hovered over the collection of books, muttering the titles to herself. Finally, she snapped her fingers, shot a hand forward, and grabbed one of the books from the lower part of the stack. "Yes. *The Storms of Martha's Vineyard*. Perhaps..." She began to flick through the pages as Kelli's heart pounded. "It's wild to think of some of these storms, isn't it? Like August 14th and 15th of the year 1635. Apparently, there was a tidal wave of more than twenty feet. Can you even imagine that? It's much larger than any of the others reported. And then, phew, Hurricane Bob? I remember that one. 1991. How old was

I then? Nine, I suppose. Ah, but here. The hurricane of 1943."

Lola propped the book up to show off the lettering, which gave the year and the month— September 1943. A black and white photo showed a crumpled-up building in Edgartown, one that neither Kelli nor Lola had ever known. Kelli drew back the first page, then the second, until she found herself gazing at a familiar sight: the Aquinnah Cliffside Overlook Hotel. There it was, in all its glory, with a number of guests positioned out front, many holding old croquet mallets. They were beautiful, high-society types— the sort that somehow had gotten out of the war, assuredly due to money or important families. The year was 1943, and the rest of the world was burning. But not there— not on Martha's Vineyard.

"They're beautiful, aren't they?" Kelli breathed, not being able to rip her eyes away from the photo.

"They just don't make people like that anymore," Lola agreed.

Beneath the line of people was a description. Kelli read the words aloud.

This photo was taken four days prior to the hurricane that ultimately tore the Aquinnah Cliffside Overlook Hotel to shreds. Listed above in order: Max Swinton and his wife, Tanya; Greta Colson and her daughter, Margaret; Henry Maddocks; Robert Sheridan; James Peterson and his wife, Marilyn.

"Oh my God. Oh my God!" Kelli cried out. Her finger found James Peterson in the photograph. He was terribly handsome with a wicked smile and eyes that seemed to know something, something almost sinister, even in their humor. Kelli's heart shattered as she gaped at this man— this man who had come to ruin her so, so long after the fact of his life. For sure, this man was now dead. All of them were.

"But— Kelli..." Lola's eyes bugged out. "His wife, Marilyn."

"Marilyn Peterson." Kelli furrowed her brow as the realization took over her. "You don't think?"

Lola lifted her own finger toward Robert Sheridan— who, Kelli recognized now, was her grandfather, a man she had never met.

A man who had worked alongside his wife, Marilyn, in operation of the Sunrise Cove Inn, until their early deaths, even before Wes and Kerry's marriages to their spouses.

Kelli's hands dropped to her sides. She felt as though she'd just uncovered an enormous secret, something buried under the sand for decades and meant to remain there. It was an incredibly important piece of their lineage, their family tree.

"Grandma was married before Grandpa," Kelli breathed. "And gosh, look at her. She was so beautiful, wasn't she?"

In the photo, her husband at the time, James, had an arm wrapped around her shoulder. Her eyes seemed to tell a story, one Kelli was ill-equipped to understand. Lola's eyes filled with tears as she continued to stare at the photo.

"Even now, as we live in the year 2021, it's difficult to be a woman. It's a man's world, and it always has been. How do you think she found her way to Grandpa? It must have been so heart-wrenching. It must have torn her apart," Lola breathed. She then swallowed the lump in her throat and added, "Do you think she loved James?"

Kelli shook her head. "I don't know. All Mom and

your dad have ever talked about is how much love they had for one another. Uncle Wes said once it was like they never needed either of their kids. 'We were just baggage holding them back,' he said, I think. Of course, he was teasing, but still, I can't imagine that. My love for Mike dried up so long ago; I don't even feel its shadow any longer. But our kids are my world."

"I think that's why they died around the same time," Lola offered. "One couldn't go on in this world without the other."

Kelli's smile faltered slightly. She lifted her phone and took a photo of the photograph within the book for safekeeping. She then texted the photo to Frederick Bachman with the words: "You were right. I just needed to do a little digging. Found my first clue!"

Frederick Bachman didn't write back immediately. In fact, he probably wouldn't even look at his phone for a number of hours.

Suddenly, Kelli remembered something: the diary tucked away in her mother's chest upstairs in the attic.

"I didn't even look at the dates. I didn't imagine at all that Grandma would come into the story," she breathed as she explained this to Lola. "But it makes sense why the old blueprints were there. Why…"

"Yes, but then why is James Peterson now listed as the owner of the hotel?" Lola demanded.

"I don't know. Maybe we can pin this down with more details from the diary."

Lola then snapped her fingers. "And that old man I interviewed who used to work with his father at the hotel! Dexter Collington! Maybe he has some memory of these people."

"Where does he live?" Kelli whispered. She now felt

like a child on a treasure hunt— reckless and willing to do anything to complete the story.

"He's in the nursing home," Lola affirmed. "But I got chummy with one of the workers so that I could interview him for the article. It shouldn't be a problem to stop by on the way to your parents' place."

As Kelli rose and began to gather her things, Max wailed from his crib. Lola bent over to calm him as Kelli's phone buzzed. It was as though time itself had sped up and tilted them toward chaos.

> XANDER VAN TRESS: Hey, I haven't heard from you. What do you say we meet this week to finalize the sale and discuss future building plans?

"Shoot." Kelli dropped her phone back on the desk as Lola turned to look at her, incredulous.

"What is it?" Lola asked.

"I just feel we're losing time," Kelli affirmed. "Let's get to the bottom of this. At least then, I can give Xander the entire story. No matter which direction it takes us. At least it's the truth. They're always saying the truth sets you free."

"If it doesn't destroy you," Lola said as she slipped baby Max into his carrier. Slowly, his cries calmed. He'd just wanted to be held for a moment, to remember how much he was cared for. Kelli could relate.

"I'll drive," Kelli said. "Let's hit the road."

Chapter Sixteen

September 17th

The Aquinnah Cliffside Overlook Hotel cowered against a frantic windstorm. Rain splattered across the window panes as Marilyn cupped her elbows with tired hands and quivered with fear. She had avoided breakfast and lunch, telling James that she felt ill and needed to keep to herself. James had told her that he felt she did, in fact, look very ill— and he knew better than to take her anywhere in such a state.

Of course, Marilyn knew that it would be a blessing to him to ensure he didn't latch himself to a pale, exhausted wife, especially as he wanted to lend a good impression to the other guests of the Cliffside Overlook. Although he hadn't yet purchased the hotel, the sort of company he'd taken up the previous weeks would almost certainly lead to numerous business dealings and, most likely, raucous nights which would involve women, lots and lots of women; women called in for the duty of doing whatever it was businessmen wanted random women to do. Marilyn knew enough about the state of the world to know this.

But it didn't matter to her what James Peterson did in his free time or any of his time, really. Her head was heavy with thoughts of Robert and how she felt she'd lost one of the most fascinating, beautiful, and nuanced relationships of her life. She had scribed endless visions of her emotions in her diary, almost praying that James would pick it up and discover the innermost aching of her soul. James wasn't a terribly curious person; more than that, he didn't imagine she had a single creative thought in that head of hers.

Perhaps she would be this miserable for the rest of her life. She needed to prepare for that— for finding unique pleasure in very small moments of her life. Perhaps she could take up needlepoint or write poetry. Perhaps she would love her children with wild intensity, so much so that she could avoid thinking about the loss of Robert. Perhaps she would think of him exactly once in the future, on her deathbed as the world faded from her vision and she fell into darkness.

The door flew open like an enormous mouth screaming out. James flung himself through it like a force of nature. In his hand, he held several sheets of paper. His expression was exuberant.

"I did it, Marilyn. I made that bastard sell me the hotel!"

Marilyn's eyes widened. She stood on wavering legs. "You're kidding."

"I'm not," he continued. "I demanded it of him a final time, and he said he would draw up the paperwork now.

That's the thing about us Peterson men, my darling. We always get what we want."

Marilyn reached a quivering hand out to take the paperwork. Sure enough, James had signed himself as the owner of the Aquinnah Cliffside Overlook Hotel, dated September 17th.

"It's everything we wanted, darling," James continued. His breath was hot with liquor. "We can stay on the island. You can reside in this very room if you like. Or perhaps we'll have a mansion built on the property to ensure we're close by. We can live between the city and the island— just as you like! And our children will know the adventures of the island and the artistry of the city."

It was almost enough, Marilyn thought then. It was nearly a perfect recipe, perhaps better than she could have dreamt when she'd first told James Peterson, "I do."

But did this mean that Robert still wanted to keep up their affair?

She now imagined decades of their lives together. She would still have James to ensure the money would continue to weave its way toward her parents, with her sneaking off to find her lover, Robert, even as she cared for James' children and performed the duties of a perfect wife.

Perhaps even some of the children wouldn't belong to James at all.

"Darling, say something!" James cried.

With that, another wind pummeled at the glass. James' eyes grew sinister and strange. He stepped toward the window and stared at the ever-darkening skies. In the city, James was never terrified of anything. It was strange, now, to recognize the symptoms of his fear. He was anxious, his hands wrapped tightly at the base of his back, and his shoulders cast all the way back.

"I think it's wonderful," Marilyn finally told him, although the sound of the wind obliterated her voice altogether. She supposed he didn't truly care what she thought, anyway.

James was quiet for a moment. His eyes scanned the horizon.

"Why aren't you dressed for dinner?" he finally asked.

Marilyn rushed to the wardrobe and selected her dinner outfit. "It won't take me long. I'll meet you there."

"Good. Robert and I plan to celebrate. He'll stay with me here at the hotel. Work with me as a sort of manager. Assuredly, he'll want to take all the money I give him and take off to all corners of the world. He's a handsome man with a wealth of good ideas. Perhaps he was wasted here, anyway."

"Are you suggesting you're not an ideas man?" Marilyn regretted the words almost instantly. She froze as she blinked into the mirror with her hairbrush raised.

But after a pause, James burst into laughter. "I never knew quite how funny you were, Marilyn. Really quite funny. I hope you'll share more of your humor as you find it." And with that, he ducked into the hallway and left Marilyn alone with a single task: look as beautiful as she possibly could, if only to make some sort of statement to Robert.

What statement would she make? Perhaps just: *I love you and I plan to always love you.* Perhaps that was enough.

* * *

Marilyn reached the bottom of the grand staircase. Near the wide stretch of the broad window, Robert and James stood side-by-side with cocktails in hand. They gawked at the same idea on the other side of the pane: the whirling chaos of the brewing storm. Marilyn's heart swam with panic as she steadied her smile.

She stepped toward the men and then glanced across the ballroom toward the restaurant, where the high-society guests seemed in a state of panic. The air was sinister and taut overhead. They leaned across the table and whispered, assuredly, about the weather. It was seven, and night would fall in the next few hours. What then? If the storm grew too frantic, there was nowhere else to go on this cliffside. She remembered that first day when she had leaned too far over the side and blinked down at the tumultuous churning waves below.

Probably now, they were ten times as tumultuous. She imagined them as a constant, bright white froth.

"There she is. My beautiful wife." James reached a hand to steady her, placing it at the base of her back. She longed to kick it off. "What do you say to Mr. Sheridan, now that we're the owners of this fine hotel?"

Marilyn's eyes glistened with tears, the likes of which only Robert noticed, as James hovered above her shoulder. After a pause, she said softly, "I suppose he's given you what you have craved, hasn't he?"

"And what's that?" Robert asked.

The windows rattled mere feet away. Everything seemed frantic and horrible.

"He gave you your freedom," Marilyn said.

Robert heaved a sigh. She saw it in his eyes: agreeing to the sale had nearly ripped him in two. Assuredly, he didn't believe James to be a worthy owner of the hotel, not so soon after Mr. Johnson's death.

"I will stick around, I think," Robert said. His voice was taut with emotion. "I love this old place. I want to make sure she gets through the change in management as easily as possible."

"You'll be a worthy mind to have around, I believe," James stated. He clapped his hand on Robert's shoulder and again turned his eyes toward the window. "I don't suppose this storm is anything to worry ourselves about?"

Robert's face was difficult to read.

"As the new owner of the hotel, it's essential that you tell me as much as you can about the state of things. I haven't grown accustomed to the violent nature of these ocean storms," James returned.

Yes, Marilyn wanted to add. He was a city boy with city boy hands. He wasn't accustomed to the way a storm could unravel in the blink of an eye and sweep over a farmhouse, as though God himself might strike it down.

"Shall we sit for a while? Have a glass of something?" Robert's cheeks were drained of color.

They sat. Marilyn's nostrils filled with the smell of him. When she closed her eyes, she remembered the gray shadows of his bedroom and the soft way he'd spoken to her when she had allowed him to see her— truly see her for the first time. James couldn't have understood the inner chaos of her soul. Instead, he ordered them a bottle of whiskey, announcing that they would soon toast to their future at the Cliffside Overlook.

The whiskey was poured. Marilyn regarded it as a safe evacuation. If she could only drink enough, maybe her annoyance at James would fade away; maybe she wouldn't remember the horror that awaited her for the rest of her days. James lifted his glass and beckoned for Robert and Marilyn to do the same.

"To us and to wherever the wind — be it as powerful and frantic as this — takes us," he breathed. "I am grateful to have been brought into such a world of history and life. And I know that I will add my personality and business prowess to it in ways that will blow all previous eras of the hotel out of the water."

James then lifted the glass a tiny bit higher, nodded his head, and dunked the glass back. Marilyn's eyes found Robert's for just a split-second as James's were closed. Robert's were difficult to read.

A man and his young son approached the table, then. All the color had drained from the man's cheeks. The young boy looked squeamish and held back as his father spoke.

"Mr. Sheridan, I believe we need to sound the alarms and get everyone to the safe house," the man said.

James cleared his throat as he tapped his glass back on the table. "Excuse me, sir. What is your name?"

The man balked. "I'm Collington, sir. I've worked at the hotel for years. Johnson and I ensured there was a safe house for storms like this."

James arched an eyebrow. "All this talk of Johnson. I've grown tired of hearing about him."

Mr. Collington looked exasperated. "If we don't get these people to a safe house, there's no telling what might happen. This hotel is quite old, and I believe it hasn't been appropriately stabilized in years. Please, Mr. Sheridan. Listen to reason."

James clucked his tongue. "Mr. Collington. It pains me to tell you this, but in fact, I'm the new owner of the

Cliffside Overlook. All decisions go through me as of this afternoon. Do you understand me?"

Mr. Collington's eyes nearly popped from his head. His hand found his young son's shoulder as he took a delicate step back.

"After what Johnson told you? You actually sold?" He spoke to Robert as though Robert had committed a heinous crime.

Robert's eyes fell toward the table. Marilyn quivered in shame. He'd done it for her, for them, and she couldn't even live bravely enough to throw everything away for him. Why? What was wrong with her?

"I think we will stay here," James scoffed then. He wanted to be resistant, to prove that he was stronger and braver than any other man.

"That is a foolish decision," Mr. Collington blared.

"Father, can we go?" The young boy whispered it as he tugged at his father's elbow.

"Dexter, yes. We're on our way." He lifted his heavy eyes toward Robert.

"James. It's imperative that we get these people out of here," Robert urged then.

Mr. Collington's posture shifted. He gave Robert a grateful nod. "We have a number of vehicles ready to go. We don't have many guests at the moment. We could have everyone to the safe house in maybe thirty minutes or less— before the storm really kicks off."

James glowered. "Excuse me. I believe I've already—"

But Robert thrust himself up from his chair so quickly that it knocked back against the ground behind him. "You know nothing of this island. Just listen to someone else besides that horrible little voice in the back of your head for once." He then clapped his hands violently to force the other diners to spring their attention toward him.

"Everyone. This tropical storm could soon take a turn. I believe it's essential that we make our way to a safe house. Gather whatever belongings you require and meet in the foyer in ten minutes' time. Remember— the most important thing to save is your life. We have very little time."

Chapter Seventeen

Dexter Collington was eighty-eight years old. He had this number proudly displayed on a number of birthday cards around his room at the nursing home, and he announced it plainly upon Lola and Kelli's entrance, saying, "I'm eighty-eight years old, but I keep telling you, Lola. If you want me to take you on a date, I'll do it in a heartbeat."

Lola laughed as the older man greeted her with a firm handshake, one that seemed overly powerful given his age.

"You're such a rascal, Dexter," Lola told him.

"And you! That article you wrote was beautiful. Thank you for including what I said. That older man Johnson is burned in my mind as one of the most spectacular men. He was a part of that older generation, you know— even older than my father. It's difficult to explain that to younger folk, now." His bright eyes were circled with wrinkles as though time itself had attempted to conceal their light. He nodded toward Kelli and said, "My name is Dexter Collington. And you are?"

"This is my cousin, Kelli," Lola introduced.

Kelli lifted a hand to shake Dexter's. She tried to envision him the way her grandmother had known him— a ten-year-old boy, following his father's orders as they maintained the old hotel. How sad it was that you could never dip behind a person's eyes and really see what they'd seen. It would have been better than any film.

"You're the woman trying to sell the old hotel," Dexter said. He slowly lowered himself into his chair, a grand event that made his knees crackle and pop.

"I am," Kelli replied. "But we've come up against a problem with the place. You see— I never knew who the owner was after Johnson. I was always told the hotel belonged to our family, that it was ours to sell. But it seems there was a final sale around the time of the hurricane. Do you know anything about that?"

Dexter's eyes were endlessly curious, like the eyes of kindergartens as you marched past their classroom. Maybe that kind of curiosity never died if you allowed it to flourish, if you continued to ask questions and live vibrantly in the world.

"There was a man on that last night," Dexter breathed. "He was so angry. Speaking to Robert, saying he owned the place."

Kelli and Lola's eyes flashed with intrigue.

"So the hotel belonged to Robert?" Kelli demanded.

"Yes. Well, Johnson left it to him. My father always said Robert didn't really know what he was doing. That was a huge burden to him. But Robert had loved Johnson like a father and really pushed himself to keep the old place afloat. It was an act of love, you see, which was why my father and I were so confused at the sale."

Kelli sputtered. "Why did he sell it to this man? And

do you remember a woman there with them?"

Dexter's eyes swam with confusion. "There was a woman, yes. I had seen her several times throughout her stay. She was married to the man who took over the hotel, I believe." His voice lowered for a moment as he added, "Always such a sad woman."

Kelli and Lola exchanged glances again. "What happened after the hurricane?" Kelli asked.

"Well, the place was completely demolished, as you know," Dexter explained. "At some point, Robert met with my father to ask that he keep tabs on the property, you know, to try to keep trespassers away. There was always hope that he would rebuild the place."

"But why wasn't James involved in the rebuilding?" Kelli asked.

"I can't tell you. I don't believe I ever saw that man again after the storm," Dexter said sadly.

"But you kept tabs on Robert over the years, didn't you?" Lola asked. Her voice ached with intrigue. In the little swaddle around her, baby Max cooed.

"Of course. My father loved Robert. I came to love him, as well. He took over the Sunrise Cove from his parents and he and his wife— well. I suppose you know all about that and their children, Wesley and Kerry."

"I'm Kerry's daughter," Kelli affirmed.

Dexter's eyelids widened. "It's always a family affair on this island, isn't it? Generations after generations, all stacked up on this beautiful rock. My daughter and two sons had children of their own, who've now had children of their own. One of those children even had a baby a few months back— even brought the baby in here to meet me. All I could think was that I wished my dad was here to see this." He chuckled.

There was a moment's pause as they each collected their thoughts. They were so far down memory lane; Kelli worried they wouldn't weave their way back to reality.

"But you must have noticed that the woman Robert was married to, the one who worked with him at the Sunrise Cove, was the very woman who'd been married to that horrible man who'd bought the hotel?" Kelli asked softly.

Dexter's smile was infectious. "I didn't notice at all. In my memory, Robert's wife was constantly laughing, chasing after little Wes and Kerry with all the energy in the world. Such a shame they died so young. Their funerals were only months apart." He lifted a handkerchief and tapped the side of his eye.

Probably, at his age, he'd been to more funerals than he knew what to do with.

"But no. I never connected that this other man's wife and Robert's wife were one and the same," he continued, his eyes alight. "She seemed a bright light of energy. Robert loved her to pieces, and she loved him right back. What more could we ever want on this earth? Don't you agree?"

A few minutes later, little Max began to really cry. Lola and Kelli stepped out of Dexter's nursing home room with copious words of thanks and many promises to return.

"I get fewer and fewer visitors over the years," he told them as he leaned on his cane. "But I have so many stories. I hope they don't get buried."

"We'll collect them, Dexter," Lola assured him as her hand spread out across Max's forehead. "You've lived quite a life through so many different eras of this island's history. Thank you for your words."

Chapter Eighteen

Mr. Collington tore down the little driveway that led toward the foyer of the Cliffside Overlook Hotel. The rain hung in sheets between Marilyn and James and the approaching vehicle. The vehicle's tires squelched through the mud and tossed mud back, splattering the car. James shifted his weight and grumbled.

"I think it might pass soon," he said of the storm.

Marilyn's throat was tight. After a strange pause, she asked, "How much did you pay Robert? For the hotel?"

James scoffed and shoved his hands deeper into his pockets. It struck Marilyn that she and James stood on a sort of sinking ship. She was reminded of that long-ago story, passengers atop the Titanic as it sank into the Atlantic, and how they'd yearned for a ship that was unsinkable. How bizarre that you couldn't believe anyone when they said they had told you the truth.

Mr. Collington beckoned for James and Marilyn to come. Marilyn had packed a single suitcase with her essentials— her jewelry, a few items of clothing that she especially liked, and, of course, her diary. James had packed nothing and had put up a hissy fit when she'd begun to pack some things for him. "It will pass!" he'd screamed to her, even as the wind had howled outside.

Mr. Collington's son sat in the front seat of the vehicle. He'd donned a little hat, which was now soaked through from the rain and dripping off the brim. Marilyn sat as far as she could away from James in the backseat. Her eyes traced the outline of the beautiful mansion as they skidded away from the property and toward the safe house. Something in her gut told her she'd never see it again. It was almost like the feeling she'd had when she'd left her parents' house to marry James in the city. She'd yearned to trace the outline of those trees forever, to capture the scent of the grass and the flowers in a vial she could return to again and again.

The safe house was located on a far hill overlooking the rest of the Vineyard to ensure no flooding. It had been built squat and low, dipped slightly into the ground beneath for stability, and it had been filled nearly to the brink with food and water for this very occasion. As Marilyn and James ducked in, one of the restaurant workers said, "I never imagined we'd ever actually need this space." Marilyn felt this was a perfect summation of the feeling of needing a safe house. You never assumed it would come to this. Always, you assumed your life would keep on carrying through, scheduled out, plotted, and schemed. Nature and life had other plans for you, always.

James and Marilyn were taken to a circular table in the far corner of the safe house. The area was dark and smoky, as many people had begun to smoke cigars and cigarettes, their motions panicked and their puffs aggressive. Marilyn had never liked smoking; her knees had always clacked together in the wake of each inhale. Now, James had no words for her; he only had fear for himself and all the money he'd just poured into this hotel, a hotel located with its face out to sea and its arms wide open to whatever horrors nature wanted to put upon it.

Where was Robert? Marilyn stirred in doubt as her eyes scanned table after table, on the hunt for that familiar, beautiful face. The wind now sounded like a torrential scream. She shivered and beckoned for one of the restaurant workers to come.

"Can you please get my husband and I some whiskey to calm our nerves?" she asked the server.

The man nodded and then promptly returned with two glasses and a bottle of whiskey. James growled that he didn't need to calm himself, that he wasn't worried at all. Still, he poured two fingers' worth of whiskey into his glass and hardly noticed when she served herself. The whiskey calmed her nerves; it brought some logical thought.

Robert still felt like the owner of the hotel. Probably, he felt his allegiance to Johnson and all he'd done more now than ever. He wouldn't seek his own safety until every last person from the hotel remained latched inside the safe house. Sweat billowed up across Marilyn's neck. She couldn't bear the thought of something happening to him.

Please. If you must take something, take the hotel. Spare Robert. Please.

She wasn't entirely sure who she said these words to. She knew better than to assume any of her asks from God or from the universe would go answered. Still, she had to think them; she hummed them over and over, crafting a sort of mantra—these words allowed for only the occasional spike of panic.

James poured himself another drink and growled inwardly. His eyes churned toward Marilyn menacingly. He then beckoned for another hotel guest to come forward. The man's name was Henrik, and he was a French immigrant, staying at the hotel until he could decide whether to remain on the island or move elsewhere. He was Jewish and had escaped before the Nazis had invaded. It didn't feel like a particularly good time to bring that up.

"How are you, my boy?" Henrik asked. "Rumor has it you just purchased that hotel we just abandoned like a burning house."

James glowered at him. He then tapped his glass and gestured for a server to bring another. He poured Henrik a glass and lifted his to cheers.

"What a ruckus this all is, hmm?" he said to Henrik. "My wife is terribly worried. And for what? Storms pass all the time. That hotel has been standing in that location for over one hundred years. God won't reach his hand down and rip it up now. Not so soon after I've put the land in my name. Besides, what is it I always tell you, Henrik?"

"You tell me that you get whatever you please," Henrik replied. He said it with the slightest dose of irony, although Marilyn sensed that James didn't pick up on it. "But what good is a world where so many men assume they always get what they please?" He said these words to Marilyn.

And at this, James erupted with laughter. He shot his elbow into Henrik as he cried, "You're a funny man, Henrik. One of the greatest. Perhaps you can stay on the island with us. I'll put you in charge of something or other. Hell, maybe you can build us up a French quarter on the island. People adore all that French stuff, don't they?"

Henrik's nose quivered. Marilyn felt she could have disappeared into her chair. She was so embarrassed at her husband's idiocy. Her fingers twitched to grab her pen and diary and start scribing all her anxious thoughts as they swirled around in her head, but it would have to wait.

Suddenly, Robert burst in through the safe house door. With him came an enormous burst of wind. Papers fluttered everywhere as many women gasped. Robert's face reminded Marilyn of men she'd seen in photographs, men who had gone to war and returned having lost something, something either physical or internal they could never get back.

She couldn't resist him. She took a huge gulp of whiskey and burst to her feet. She hustled through the crowd, her thin legs weaving around others' knees and awkward skirts. Perhaps James had cried out for her to stop; she couldn't have heard him over the rush of the wind and the wild, provocative conversation.

When she reached Robert, she placed her hands on his upper arms and watched as he folded up against her, gasping. His forehead was plastered against her shoulder; his dark hair spilled over her neck. Her hand swept over his drenched hair as she whispered, "It's going to be all right, Robert. It's going to be all right."

Her heart shattered as he shifted his head from left to right, a firm NO. Slowly, he lifted his chin so that his eyes connected with hers.

"It just crumbled," he breathed. "I watched it as I

raced off the land. A tree barreled against a part of it, and the whole structure of it crumbled. Even the dome over the ballroom— it was cast inward. The sound of it was horrible. The worst thing you can imagine. I finally turned to watch the road and nearly drove myself off a cliff. I wasn't paying attention."

Marilyn's heart seized with terror. She placed her hand over his cheek and brought his face up so that he stood tall once more.

"I nearly lost you," she whispered.

He shook his head. "I wasn't going to let that happen. But the hotel, it's gone."

As the safe house was entirely too loud, a chaotic collection of bodies screaming over one another, nobody had heard Robert's somber tale. But suddenly, James appeared between others' heads. His cheeks were bright red, the stuff of an alcoholic's face, and he leered at the two of them until Marilyn dropped her hands to her sides. Again, horror latched around her heart. How could she describe the reason why she'd flung herself toward Robert without pause and placed her hands over his cheeks?

"I can see it all over your face," James seethed then, his voice low.

But he didn't speak to Marilyn. He spoke instead to Robert.

"It collapsed, didn't it?" James's words were sinister, laced with alcohol. One of his hands formed a fist.

Robert's eyes were rimmed with tears, but he wouldn't allow them to fall.

"You knew this would happen," James breathed then.

"No. How could I have possibly known?" Robert demanded.

"You knew. And you didn't just want to rob me. You

also wanted to make a fool out of me. Go to hell, Robert." He then turned his eyes toward Marilyn, who quivered, essentially there between them. "And you. You ignorant, foolish woman," he grumbled. "I'm taking you back to the city where you belong. I don't know what kind of fantasy you've built up in your head. But you and me, we're two peas in a pod. If you don't see it, you're much stupider than even I thought."

Marilyn gasped. Robert lifted his fist. Overwhelmed with emotion, with James far too drunk to make any rash motions or react instinctively, Robert barreled his fist into James's chin. James was tossed back into the table directly behind him. A lady screeched as her wine flew over her dress and across her blond hair. James collapsed in a heap; his legs coiled over themselves as he fell into some kind of stupor.

"Get him up! Get him up!" Marilyn cried.

Two waiters hurried over and lifted poor, foolish James from the wreckage. They splayed him in the corner as Marilyn sat alongside him and attempted to stop the bleeding on the side of his head. She demanded water, and Robert shot forth with a bucket of it. But when she discovered that James was very much alive and very much too drunk to be more conscious than this, she placed a pillow under his head and returned to Robert's side.

Robert glared at the ground. He tossed his foot to and fro beneath him. Slowly, Marilyn slipped her fingers through his and heaved a sigh.

"You can't go around punching people like that, Robert," she told him.

"I've wanted to punch him since I met him, to be fair with you," he returned.

Marilyn's heart lifted. She couldn't glance up to find

Robert's eyes. The intensity of holding hands in this public space, with her husband sleeping off his drink only a few feet away, was electrifying. She felt she might rise off the floor very soon.

"How long do these hurricanes last, anyway?" she asked.

"Hmm. Sometimes twelve hours. Sometimes twenty-four. Sometimes more," Robert reported.

Marilyn sighed. "I suppose it'll be a very, very long night."

Robert wrapped his arms around her and held her against him. His hand wrapped over her head as tears slipped down her cheeks. She knew now that she would never leave Martha's Vineyard— not without Robert beside her. She would manage to find a way to send money to her family. If there was a will and enough love to go around, there was a way.

Chapter Nineteen

When Kelli and Lola pulled up at the Montgomery house a little while later, they found themselves facing more than ten vehicles, all of which belonged to either family or friends. Lola muttered, "I swear, every day in this family is a day of celebration. Can't they just give it a rest? Aunt Kerry's slaved away in the kitchen all summer long."

Kelli laughed. "I can't imagine taking on that role. All those barbecues we'll have to plan in the future just to keep this big Montgomery-Sheridan ship running?"

"I'm going to pass it on to Audrey and Lexi and Amanda," Lola affirmed. "No way am I making endless varieties of snack trays for hungry islanders. Not even if I love them to bits."

Lola retrieved Max from his carrier as Kelli assembled her folder of the old deed along with the blueprint and the old book from the library. She had within her a seed of information that, when planted, could generate a plethora of emotions, especially within her mother. How lucky Kelli now felt, suddenly, that she'd been able to have her mother all these years. Kerry had lost Marilyn far, far too early. They'd been robbed of decades of love.

"There they are!" Lexi hollered from the side of the living room, where she sat with her cousin, Jonathon, who was Steven's oldest. She beckoned for her mother and then, when she was in earshot, said, "I sold another top-ticket item from the boutique today. One of those stewardess suitcases from the seventies."

"Honey, that's fantastic," Kelli breathed. "I can't believe it. You've already sold more in the past week than I managed to sell all summer long." She dropped and kissed her daughter on the head, suddenly overwhelmed with love for her.

Lexi's nostrils curled upward. "What's up, Mom? You look pale."

"Guess I just haven't eaten," Kelli said. "Have you seen your grandmother?"

"She's in the kitchen, of course," Jonathon interjected. "With Charlotte and Claire."

Although she loved them deeply and felt protective over them, Kelli had always felt a kind of distance from her younger sisters. Charlotte and Claire were chummy and had always been. Decades earlier, Kelli had scolded them for giggling deep into the night when she and her older brother had needed sleep for various high school tests or high school competitions. They'd had an energy and a liveliness to them, even all those years ago, that Kelli had coveted.

"Hey there, big sis!" Claire greeted her as she sliced through an onion. "Everyone wondered where you were. I said you were off doing what you do best. Being superwoman and all that." Again, she sliced the knife through the vegetable.

"Have you made the final deal yet?" Kerry asked from the fridge. "With Xander, I mean. Or did you manage to —" She grimaced as her eyes fell. "You haven't sold it. You let your feelings get in the way, didn't you?"

"Feelings?" Charlotte demanded. "What feelings?"

"She's been seeing this client of hers. I told her it would get her into all sorts of trouble, but what do I know?" Kerry asked as she flung her hands back. She then scurried for the bottle of wine, which she flipped upside down over a wine glass.

"Mom! It isn't about that," Kelli insisted. Her cheeks were flushed, showing how annoyed she was.

"So you haven't been seeing him?" Claire asked, her eyes mischievous. "And Mom. Why wouldn't you want Kelli to see someone? She's been through hell and back."

"Please, don't say curse words to your mother," Kerry scolded, clearly exasperated.

It was just the same sort of dynamic they'd always had. Kerry had fallen into a state of exhaustion.

"Besides, you know how we feel about that old property. We've longed to sell it for as long as we've been in the real estate business. You got this close, Kelli. This close!" Kerry's eyes widened with shock. "I just can't believe you—"

"Now, wait just a minute," Kelli balked. She'd had another memory of Mike from long ago, using the same exact tone with her— belittling her in ways she had never assumed she would allow herself to be belittled. Was it possible that this initial accosting had come from her mother? And she'd just allowed it to go on with her husband?

Maybe, in the slightest way, Kerry had created the first tear that had allowed the floodgates to open upon

Mike's arrival into her life. But parents weren't perfect; Kelli knew this after her own pitfalls as a mother.

And suddenly, Kelli whipped out the old book and tore through the pages until she found the old photograph. She pointed at the image and followed her mother's gaze.

"What on earth is this?" Kerry demanded.

"Just look. And read the description," Kelli insisted. "Before you belittle me again."

Kerry turned her eyes over every face until she stopped short at the image of the woman off to the right.

"Mom," she breathed, for she naturally recognized the woman's face in an instant. "Wow. Look at her. She looks so beautiful here. So regal and powerful."

Kelli's heart shattered. There was such love and curiosity behind her words.

"And look, Mom," Kelli pointed at the description beneath. "She was married. To someone called James Peterson."

Kerry's eyes widened. "No, that can't be. That's Dad right there."

"But it says here that she is James Peterson's wife, Marilyn."

Kerry balked. "It's impossible. It must be a typo."

Kelli then whipped out the old deed as she attempted to explain the events of the previous weeks. "I don't think that old place really belongs to our family, Mom. Look. A lawyer who represents the family of James Peterson arrived to give me this— proof that we can't legally sell it."

Kerry stuttered. "Dad always said it was up to us to take care of it. He'd hired that guy, Dexter, to keep it up after his father passed. I just can't understand this, Kelli. I really don't know what to say."

"We just spoke with Dexter at his nursing home," Kelli said hurriedly as she pointed out toward Lola, who nodded from the living room as she bobbed baby Max around. "And he said James had a wife with him— an unhappy wife. He never even realized she was the same woman who Robert eventually married."

Kerry continued to shake her head. "I don't understand. I can't even..." She trailed off.

"I think we should look at her diaries," Kelli suggested then. "It's the only way to really know what happened."

Kerry's chin quivered slightly. She reached out for Claire's hand and clutched it hard so that Claire let out a strange animal sound of pain.

"My darling mother died far too young. And then, my father followed in her footsteps. Wes and I weren't sure what to do without them. I've never felt like that diary was mine to read, you know? I never wanted to invade her privacy. But I suppose it's time to really dig in. Find some answers." She closed her eyes as a tear rolled down her cheek. She then glanced toward the unprepared food, the sliced onions, and the water heating on the stove.

"And we're ordering pizza for anyone who asks," Kerry announced then before she walked into the hallway and headed for the stairs.

En route to the attic, Kelli nearly ran headlong into her brother, Andy. She'd hardly seen him throughout the past few weeks since his engagement. Here, she threw her arms around him, heaved a sigh, and said, "I have so much to tell you. There are some pretty crazy family secrets coming to a head."

"Uh oh. Some skeletons in our closet?"

"Something like that," Kelli affirmed before she hustled after her mother.

Despite her seventy-two years, Kerry scurried up that ladder and headed straight for the chest before any of her daughters could reach it.

"Don't bother coming up! I'll just grab it and come back down," Kerry called. "And did someone call for pizza, or do I also have to do that, too?"

Claire disappeared to ask Russell to take orders and make the call. After that, Kelli, Kerry, Claire, and Charlotte all piled onto Kerry and Trevor's bed with the diary between them. It felt fitting that it was the four of them— the daughters of the daughter of the woman in question— the mystery woman of their past.

"I don't even know where to start," Kerry whispered.

"I think we should head to the time right after the storm," Kelli suggested. "Around mid to end of September 1943."

Kerry flicked through the pages as tears formed in her eyes. But when she reached September, the diary pages stopped from September 16 to September 30.

"What! No," Kelli cried.

This felt like the pulsing heartbeat of everything else, the era when her grandmother had made some of the biggest decisions of her life. Yet perhaps, those sorts of decisions didn't always make their way onto the page. Perhaps they existed only in the heart.

"Maybe start where she begins again after the hurricane?" Claire asked.

"Okay. Sure." Kerry cleared her throat and began to read.

September 30, 1943

You can't imagine how pleased I am to have been rid of so many of the fine clothes James forced me to wear as his high-society wife. The storm ensured they were gone for good, and in their wake, I have only a smattering of things I've collected, mostly from Robert's sister and mother. One dress is something his mother wore when she was pregnant with him, and it's monstrous on me. I look like the country tom-girl I always knew myself to be. I asked Robert if he finds me less attractive now that he sees me in such rags. He says, on the contrary, he always knew me to be rough around the edges. At this, I always give him a little punch on the arm.

He's sad, to say the least, about the hotel. We went up last night to see how the clearing of much of the wreckage has gone. Some of the rubble and stones will be used in other areas of the island; others will be taken to a scrapyard. It's strange to see over one hundred years of history torn apart like this in just one day.

I asked Robert if he might like to use the property to build something back up. But he says that old place was always too much for him, anyway. The Sunrise Cove was built by his parents, and he longs to take it over one day. It is a quaint little place, beautiful and cozy. I've already asked his mother if I might be able to help with some of the cooking duties at their little restaurant. She was surprised, as she'd heard I was a high-society girl from the big city. I explained that, in reality, I am a farm girl, unafraid of hard work. I think she's pleased Robert found himself someone like that.

I do wonder what will become of James.

At this, Kerry screeched and flung the diary down. Her cheeks were lined with tears.

"I just can't believe this," she breathed. "So much about my mother I never knew— this whole other life. High society! What on earth and for how long? And what did she actually think of this James fellow?" Kerry continued to shake her head as Claire splayed her hand over her shoulder and began to massage it.

"Maybe we can take turns reading from it?" Charlotte offered.

"She's such a beautiful writer," Claire agreed. "I just love hearing her words."

"But where on earth is this James Peterson? And why did she leave him?" Kerry asked as her voice broke.

Charlotte flipped a bit forward in the book to an entry from mid-July.

August 14, 1943

We've been married for only a month now and already I see the cracks in our union.

Mother told me I had to remain strong in the face of whatever duties James insists for me to do. I find myself studying his face as he sleeps, dreaming of ways to slip out in the middle of the night. Perhaps I will run to Times Square and scream up at the sky— scream and scream until someone takes me away to the psych ward and I am freed from this horrible nightmare that I can't wake from.

For I've never met a more childlike man. His way is the only way. He imagines I think of nothing, attributes no sense of creativity within me. I haven't laughed since I walked down the aisle.

Yet, I remind myself that this is what my life's work is. I am a woman, and thusly, I must pledge to care for my family. I say their names as I slip off to sleep at night and again when I awake in the morning. They are my everything.

"Mom, she was so much like you," Kelli said then. "Putting her family above everything else."

This made Kerry cry all the more. Her shoulders sagged at the tremendous weight of it all. Charlotte dropped her head onto her mother's shoulder, and together, the two generations of Montgomery girls cried over the Sheridan girl they had lost forever, who'd given everything to save her family— and still managed to save herself and her love in the end.

Chapter Twenty

The following morning, Kelli stood in a half-daze in the hazy light of her kitchen as the coffee maker bubbled its black juices into the base of the pot. It was seven-thirty, just as it always seemed to be, and upstairs, Lexi padded around in preparation for her rush to the boutique. In some respects, Kelli could pretend that this was any other day in any other portion of her life. In reality, Sam and Josh were no longer home; Mike was far away, a labeled abuser, and an actual poor excuse for a man. Time had been cruel to her in several ways— and it had tossed her into this life alone. Maybe she'd needed it to learn a thing or two.

Lexi rushed into the kitchen, a flurry of color, of vintage garb she'd hand-selected from the boutique, saying, "I need to look the part of a cool girl if I'm going to sell clothing to cool girls, Mom." Despite the sassiness of her words, Kelli agreed with her.

"My little businesswoman," Kelli chirped, brimming with pride.

"Ha." Lexi paused as she adjusted her jean vest with

its brightly painted buttons. She slowly dragged her eyes back to her mother's. "Are you doing okay? After last night? I thought Grandma would never stop crying."

Kelli sighed. "It was a whole lot of information for all of us."

Lexi nodded knowingly. "To me, I'm just pleased to know that we have such strong women in our family. Women who reach out for what they need when they need it. And in 1943! That must have been so much harder to do. Anyway, this isn't related at all, but I do want to say that I've been thinking about what I want to do this fall because, you know, I did graduate from high school."

Kelli laughed. "I know. I was there. I have about four hundred photos to prove it."

Lexi rolled her eyes. How much longer would she show off these teenager tropes? Perhaps they would float away from her soon when she had children of her own and learned the weight they brought upon your heart and your shoulders.

"I would really like to sign up for business classes," Lexi continued. "Alongside managing the boutique, I looked at some online classes out of Boston College. They look cool. Management and advertising and marketing, things like that. Maybe I can fill my head with actual knowledge instead of just the pages of *Seventeen* magazine for a change. What do you think?"

Kelli's heart brimmed with pride.

"Aw, come on, Mom. Don't look at me like that," Lexi offered, blushing. "Let's just talk about it later. I have to run."

"Wait—" Kelli called as Lexi stepped out of the screen door.

But at that moment, Kelli's phone buzzed with proof of bigger fish to fry.

> XANDER VAN TRESS: I hope you're not ghosting me.

Her heart dropped into her stomach. How celebratory that all had been! How she'd longed to draw up the paperwork for Xander Van Tress to purchase the property at the Cliffside Overlook. She had even thought she might help him with the reconstruction, lending over the blueprints and hand-selecting period-appropriate wallpaper. She was certainly an optimist, despite all the universe's best efforts against it.

Kelli inhaled sharply and drummed up that long-lost Sheridan-Montgomery women's confidence. She lifted her phone and dialed his number and listened to two, then three rings as he probably stared at his phone, wondering what the hell she was doing.

Xander's voice sounded cold, almost sinister.

"Hey there."

Kelli remembered that glittering day upon the Nantucket Sound as she'd stood, so barren, in just her bikini with her chin lifted as the sun had billowed up countless freckles across her nose. He'd said he liked them.

Was this the same man?

Had she ruined everything with her silence and fear?

"Xander. Hi. I have a lot to tell you," Kelli said. It was better to be straightforward, wasn't it? Even if he wanted nothing to do with her. At least then, she could say what she wanted to say and be done with it without any lingering doubts.

They decided to meet at the Sunrise Cove Inn Bistro.

It felt appropriate to do it there, where Marilyn had found peace all those years before. Kelli jumped in the shower and allowed the steam to billow through the room; the piping-hot water became like razors across her back. She turned off the water and stood lost in her thought. What a strange journey this all had been.

Her car window's reflection gave her a final view of herself prior to their lunch meeting. Her hair looked curly and a tiny bit wild— as it had that day on the sailboat and her neckline was slightly too low, proof that maybe she wasn't dead just yet, that, in fact, she wanted things far more than words could say. She wore a long skirt with gladiator sandals and gold bangles that jangled on her wrist. Had she worn something like this with Mike, he'd have told her she looked like a working girl. But in fact, she just looked like every other fashionable woman on the Vineyard.

Mike knew nothing. But then again, it was thanks to Mike that they'd learned all of this about Marilyn Sheridan. So wasn't that something?

Xander was seated at the corner table in the Sunrise Cove Inn Bistro. He sipped a mimosa and leaned back steadily in his chair. His chin lifted toward the glass window, and his eyes were seemingly captivated by the rolling waves. That was the thing about the ocean. You could look at it endlessly and never grow tired of it.

"Xander. Hi." Kelli paused at the table before she sat.

When Xander's eyes found her, she knew instantly that the outfit was a success. He gave her that playful smile, as though all was forgiven, and stood to greet her with a tender kiss on the cheek. They were friendly, if nothing else. Now, it was up to her to fight for the "everything else" part.

"Thank you for meeting me," Kelli said. She sat across from him as her heart performed a tap-dance across her diaphragm. She spotted Christine toward the bakery portion of the bistro and gave a little wave. Christine immediately struck into action and appeared with a fresh platter of croissants and a new pitcher of mimosa.

"Family gets treated like kings and queens around here," Christine told Xander. "You're in luck to be with a Montgomery girl."

Xander's smile was infectious. "I remember her from your family get-togethers. Killer baker. I think she told me she's worked across the world."

Kelli nodded. "My sisters and I were pretty jealous. She was in Paris and Stockholm but mostly New York. But I think she struggled for a long time to find herself."

Xander nodded tentatively. "All that chasing after something can kill you. Especially in the city."

Kelli's heart shifted with sorrow. She imagined Xander alone, waging war on his life without anyone who truly loved him around.

"I take it you and your father weren't always together as a partnership?"

"No. We were apart for many years. I think, in a sense, he saved my life." Xander shook his head as though to clear the cobwebs. "But I didn't come here to discuss myself. I came here to talk about the property, which I would still like to buy if you haven't received some kind of a better offer. To be honest, I'd just top that offer at this point. I can't imagine not owning that property. There is so much magic there. And it's been wasted for so many decades. It's heartbreaking."

Kelli dropped down and removed the book from the library and splayed it across the table between them. She flashed a finger down toward the base of the photo, where her grandmother stood.

"That's my grandma. Her name was Marilyn," Kelli started as she glanced at him then back to the picture.

Xander's eyes widened as he began to comprehend the weight of the story to come. "I see."

"In this photo, she was married to this man. James Peterson."

"But he isn't your grandfather?"

"No. This man right here is. Apparently, Robert was the owner of the hotel at the time of this photo— but ownership was passed at the last moment to James Peterson before he abruptly left the island forever. He's owned the property all this time. And nobody ever knew about this story. Not my parents, certainly, otherwise they wouldn't have been attempting to sell this place all these years."

Xander nodded firmly and sipped his mimosa.

Kelli grinned. "You're not fazed by this at all, are you."

"No. I'm not. It's an incredible story. But it doesn't change anything," Xander affirmed.

"I mean, it changes the fact that I can't sell it," she pointed out.

"Sure, but you now know who this guy is. Why can't we track him down? Figure out what he wants to do with it. It seems to me that the property has been wasted all these years, and now it's time to do something about it. We can't just sit on an old story and wait for something to happen. It's up to us to extend the storyline."

Kelli's smile faltered. The enormity of her feelings toward him was difficult to describe. She shook her head and reached across the table to slip her fingers through his. He looked almost caught off guard, but only almost.

"You don't seem afraid of anything, the way I'm afraid of stuff," Kelli said softly.

Xander gripped her fingers harder. Something exciting quivered in the base of her belly. How she longed to go home with him, to go anywhere with him. His eyes captivated her. His acceptance of life and its many inconsistencies and bizarre storylines thrilled her. She wanted to be more like him, and she wanted to love him, too.

"I gave up on feeling afraid," he whispered. "It wasn't serving me. And it isn't serving you, either."

They held one another's gaze for a long moment. Then, he nodded and said, "I think we should find James Peterson— together. Do you have any leads?"

Kelli flipped through the old folder that the lawyer had brought her. There, just as ever, was his business card. She dialed the number as Christine brought them out a wide platter of eggs, bacon, vegetables, and cheese. She left with a wink, her hand extended over her belly. Kelli's heart swelled with love.

"Hi there," Kelli announced. "My name is Kelli Montgomery, and I am very interested in speaking with your client, James Peterson."

The lawyer who had vaguely threatened her now sounded terribly professional. "The only problem with that, I'm afraid, is that he's quite deceased. You could meet with his son, however, the last remaining. He lives in New York City. Let me contact him." He paused and then admitted, "I didn't think you'd cooperate when I went all that way. I assumed I would have to take some sort of legal action. I'm a bit mystified by it all as it's rare to meet kind people who listen to reason."

The man hung up after that, leaving Kelli in a state of confusion. She pressed the phone to the side of the table and blinked back up into Xander's eyes. He wagged his eyebrows playfully and lifted his fork.

"While we wait, I guess we should eat this delicious selection of food?"

Kelli laughed. "I thought you'd never say so."

It was a rare thing to relax in front of someone enough to eat with them, especially so early on. But Kelli found herself eating voraciously, following him bite-for-bite as he told her about what he'd done to occupy his time while he assumed she was "ghosting" him.

"I hate this term," Kelli laughed. "Ghosting!"

"Yes, but you don't know what it's like out there," Xander told her. "I've dated so much in New York. Ghosting is an illness. It's pervasive."

"It sounds kind of weak. Like you do it if you're scared of something, scared of the truth," Kelli affirmed.

"That's right. And if there's anything I want to face, it's the truth," Xander said, just as the lawyer called her back.

"All right. He wants to meet. Can you be there tonight?"

Chapter Twenty-One

Christine poured them two piping-hot cups of coffee in takeaway cups and remained in the doorway of the Sunrise Cove Bistro as Xander and Kelli slipped into Xander's convertible and prepared for the journey ahead. It was just past one in the afternoon, and once they got off the ferry, New York was a five-hour drive away. As Kelli glanced at herself in the mirror, she shivered with a mix of intrigue and fear. Xander gave her a sidelong glance, to which she responded, "I haven't been off the island in over a year, if you can believe it."

Xander's smile was electric. "I'm happy to be the one to take you out into the wide world, Miss Montgomery. Shall we?"

When the ferry landed in Woods Hole, Xander shifted slowly, softly in line with the other vehicles as they rode back into the light of the summer's day. Kelli told him that growing up on the island meant you had a rather complicated relationship with the concept of tourists.

"In some respects, it feels like they swarm your home. In others, the first sight of them means good things to come. It means barbecues and sailing competitions and bonfires on the beach. It means beautiful people in luxury clothing running around with bright smiles on their faces. And most of all, it means income. It's historically when the island makes all it needs for the year ahead."

"Can't live with them, and you can't live without them," Xander recited as he slowly shifted gears and then ramped up speed, headed toward the highway that would draw them south and then west, along the coastline, toward that other island, the one of fame and glory and billions of dollars. The one where, long ago, Kelli's grandmother had resided for only a few months alongside her first husband, a man who had belittled her in much the same way Mike had belittled Kelli. How strange.

"What do you listen to on road trips, Miss Montgomery?" Xander asked.

Two or three minutes of silence had passed, during which Kelli's mind had raced with panic.

"Hmm. You're leaving this important choice up to me?"

Xander shrugged. "It's a test."

"Oh, wonderful. I love tests," Kelli said. She flicked around the stations until she landed on an old tune that she'd always loved.

"Ah. A deep-cut Nirvana?" Xander's eyes glittered as he leaned his head against the car seat. He seemed to dip back into his old memories as his lips parted.

"I was into all of this stuff when I was younger," Kelli told him. "I guess I thought I was something of a cool girl in high school."

"Maybe you wouldn't have even looked twice at me."

Kelli laughed aloud. "I doubt that very much."

Xander lowered the volume the slightest bit as the guitar sound grew increasingly raucous. "But really. I'm curious. What were you like in high school? What would I have thought of you had I met you?"

It was a funny thing— the fact that Kelli had spent the previous days diving deep into her grandmother's past. Now, to shake off the previous thirty years of her own life, beyond the kids and the trauma of having an abusive husband, to really see herself as a teenager: was a difficult thing. She set her jaw as she visualized herself all those years ago, with a walk-man around her ears as she listened to alternative nineties music and wore her choker necklaces and thought, very much, that she had total control over her own destiny.

"I was very self-assured during those years," she finally said with a funny grin.

"What do you mean?"

"I just felt very confident. I knew what kind of music I liked. I knew what I wanted to wear. I knew that the world saw me as a beautiful and confident and youthful creature, and I used that to my advantage. I suppose that's why my husband eventually fell for me. I think he coveted what I felt, and he somehow used that, stole that power from me."

Xander's face fell. "That's a terrible story."

Kelli shrugged. "I'm just now trying to comprehend the weight of my own story— trying to add it all up in my head in a way that makes sense. I think we can slip through life without truly comprehending the things that hurt us. But I don't want to do that anymore. I want to look at everything bravely, full-on. Does that make sense? I feel like I'm talking a bit crazy."

A Vineyard Rebirth

Xander turned his head the slightest bit and removed his gaze from the road. His eyes were fully focused and clear.

"It makes so much sense, Kelli. So much sense," he told her firmly. "And your bravery makes me want to continue to fight my own instincts. Become a better person, whatever that looks like. I think every year, if you don't tap into yourself and see how you've advanced from the previous year, then you're allowing time to have its way with you."

Kelli nodded as the wind tore through her hair and across her cheeks. She imagined trying to have a similar conversation with Mike. He wouldn't have allowed it. He would have belittled this as "silly banter that is wasting precious time," then probably disappeared into the kitchen for a bag of chips and some beer. On instinct, Kelli reached over and slipped her fingers through Xander's hand. His skin was warm, and his grip was strong, powerful. She felt protected, even as they surged down this great American highway, with only the bright July sky above.

* * *

Xander's New York City apartment was located only a few blocks from Charlie Peterson's place, which allowed them to park in his extended parking in the belly of the great beast that was his high-rise apartment. Xander even knew the valet working. His keys erupted from his hand as the valet leaped for them, as though they'd performed this very action time and time again.

"I thought you'd never come back," the valet told

Xander as he tossed the keys into the air, making them jangle.

"You know I'll always be back in the city," Xander returned. He then placed a hand at the base of Kelli's back and introduced her. "This is Kelli Montgomery. She's been helping me secure a new property on Martha's Vineyard. This one came with its own share of technicalities."

"Sounds fascinating," the valet said as he wagged his eyebrows. "Good to meet you, Miss Montgomery." He then leaped into the convertible and drew a line off into the darkness, where the car would remain parked until they returned home.

It seemed incredible to Kelli that when they did return home, they would do it together, like some kind of team.

Xander led her out to the foyer of his immaculate high-rise building and greeted the doorman in a similar fashion. He again introduced Kelli, then jumped into the elevator, explaining that he wanted to check on some things, including his plants.

"I didn't know I'd have the pleasure of seeing your home," she told him as the elevator doors closed.

"It's no Vineyard," Xander affirmed. "But I have loved it all these years. It's my little oasis in the city."

"Little" was probably not the adjective Kelli might have chosen to describe the enormous apartment. She stepped into the beautiful, brightly lit space and felt blown away by the attention to detail, the iconic furniture, and the artwork that adorned the walls, assuredly worth somewhere in the millions of dollars.

Xander eased through his apartment without pause. Kelli wanted to tease him about this— that he no longer had to look at his immaculate paintings, at his glorious sculptures, as he'd grown too accustomed to them. When he paused at the counter of his kitchen, he caught her eye and gave her a funny smile.

"You must think this is all overkill," he said finally. "And admittedly, I agree with you. I went a little overboard when I first decorated the place. I was dating an art collector at the time, and I told her to really go for it."

Kelli whistled. "She followed your rule to a T."

"I was featured in several art magazines," he continued as he hunted through his cabinets, eventually procuring a small watering can. "And interviewed about my artistic eye. But in truth, I could sell half of this stuff and not blink an eye. The beauty of the place lay in the creation of it. Now that it just sits without anyone in it for most of the time, it's wasted. Art is meant to be appreciated. It's why I don't always know how to feel about art museums. Shouldn't art always be around us?"

Kelli swallowed the lump in her throat. Without pause, listening only to the instincts in her heart, she rushed across the space between them and pressed her lips against his. She wanted to be the woman he kissed in his high-rise apartment building. She wanted to be there in the silence of the afternoon, so far above the swirling chaos of the city, feeling all these things for this beautiful, intelligent man.

Kelli helped Xander with his various house duties. He explained that he had a young sister-brother duo stopping by most afternoons to water his plants and check on his fish, but that he wanted to ensure everything was going smoothly himself. It was a funny thing to watch him in his element, to fall into rhythm with him as they watered and fed and fixed everything up. At one point, Xander even put on an old Mazzy Star record from the nineties, and the two of them lay back on Xander's enormous bed and blinked at the ceiling and felt the immensity of the lyrics in their souls.

"I think it's time to head over and face the music," Xander suggested about an hour after their arrival. "Charlie's expecting us."

Kelli whistled. "My almost father."

Xander laughed. "Is that how genealogy works?"

"I believe it is," Kelli replied with a wink. She then headed for the elevator, which opened up within his apartment, like in movies. She pressed the DOWN button and crossed her arms over her chest. "It's time to face the music. I'm terrified."

Chapter Twenty-Two

Charlie Peterson was older than Kerry Montgomery by three years, which made him the same age as Mark Van Tress— seventy-five. He stood at six foot four inches, proof of what Kelli knew from the old photographs: that James had been a very tall, very dominant, and very formidable character. Probably, Marilyn had been frightened of him in some respects, a fear she'd had to overcome in leaving him.

Charlie's hair was a stark white. Despite the July heat, he wore a sweater vest and a pair of corduroys, along with a pair of circular glasses, which made him look incredibly literary. This sense matched the walls of books, which stretched out on either side of him. Kelli and Xander remained in the foyer, blocked off by this much taller, much older man.

"Good evening," Charlie greeted them. "I suppose this is about as strange for you as it is for me."

Kelli's lips quivered ever so slightly; she yearned to laugh but sensed it wasn't the appropriate time. Xander, ever the gentleman, stuck his hand out for Charlie to shake.

"Thank you for meeting us this evening," he said. "My name is Xander Van Tress. And this is Kelli Montgomery."

Charlie lifted Kelli's hand as though he planned to kiss the top, like a very old gentleman might. At the last second, he released it, then dropped his chin toward his chest.

"Please, come in. I've prepared drinks for us all. I hope you like whiskey."

Kelli and Xander sat on a leather couch which faced a matching leather chair, upon which Charlie now sat. He crossed his legs, which were altogether too thin, then gestured up toward a large photograph, which hung in a gold frame between bookshelves off to the right.

"I suppose you will recognize the man in that photograph," Charlie pointed.

Kelli lifted her chin to find James Peterson himself. In the photograph, he wore a wedding tuxedo. His hand was latched around a small, doll-sized hand, which belonged to a beautiful blond woman whose smile was as bright as the sun, almost as iconic as Marilyn Monroe's. She looked different to Kelli's Grandmother Marilyn in nearly every way, as though, once Marilyn Sheridan had left him, James had required himself to find the complete opposite in a wife.

"That is my mother," Charlie said sadly. "Rita."

"She's beautiful," Kelli offered. "As is he."

Charlie nodded. "That was the year 1945. I suppose two years after your grandmother left him."

"You can't see it on his face at all," Kelli breathed. "None of the pain of that first marriage."

"He really loved my mother," Charlie affirmed. "And perhaps against what you immediately think, he treated her wonderfully. They had a beautiful and compassionate marriage. I was born the following year, in 1946, and throughout my childhood, I remember them being a portrait of love and gratitude. My friends were mesmerized as their parents fought themselves to smithereens. Of course, as a child, I didn't know about my father's harried past, nor about Marilyn."

Kelli's throat tightened. "When did you eventually learn about her?"

Charlie's face twitched. "When I was a young man myself— I know, quite difficult to picture at this point— I fell in love with a woman named Mildred. She longed to get married on Martha's Vineyard. I told my father our plans, and he was obstinate, stating that he never would allow such an event on Martha's Vineyard. It got my head spinning in circles. I couldn't understand why my father, who had always been such a wonderful and balanced man, had created this very strict rule. Several months after this fight, Mildred left me for another man, and I fell into one of the deepest depressions of my life. This was when my father took me aside, poured me a glass of whiskey, and told me the story of Marilyn."

Kelli and Xander exchanged glances, mesmerized.

"His face was different than I'd ever seen it," Charlie continued. "It was shadowed and strange. He recounted the story of how his parents had introduced him to Marilyn and informed him that he would marry her. How she'd seemed so beautiful to him, so kind and gentle. But that he'd been a far different man back then. I couldn't understand it. He tried to explain. He said he'd been rash and arrogant. That he'd belittled her in ways he now couldn't comprehend. After Marilyn left him, he took a very hard look at his own behavior and corrected himself. The man my mother met was not the man your grandmother married and then left. That is for sure.

"But that said, just a mere mention of Martha's Vineyard had brought out this other side of my father. He was irate with himself and, over the next several years, waged war on himself about whether or not to reach out to Marilyn and ask for some sort of forgiveness. It came up only once every few months, usually if he poured me a drink and wanted to talk it out with me. I was proud of the fact that my father wanted me to be a confidant. And eventually, after I was married myself, I urged him to write Marilyn a letter. Perhaps it would calm his inner demons. He received a blessing from my mother to do it, as well, as she recognized all the pain behind my father's eyes when he thought about this portion of his life.

"But when he finally reached out, the letter received no answer. He finally called a newspaper office on Martha's Vineyard and learned that both Marilyn and her husband, Robert, had passed away. My father was devastated with this news. He took to his bed for an entire day. When he finally rose to speak with me about it, he said it simply wasn't fair— that he had been allowed this long and happy life, with his four children and his beautiful wife, and Marilyn had been taken from the world so soon."

Kelli's eyes filled with tears. How was it possible that this man had found compassion in the wake of the horror of his first marriage? Was it true that people could change so quickly?

"I believe he really loved her, in a way," Charlie

finally continued. "He always said my mother was the love of his life, and I believe she was. But Marilyn represented a love that he'd lost due to his own youthfulness and idiocy. And I don't believe he ever really got over it."

Kelli and Xander held the silence for a long moment. Out the window of the high-rise, a bird swooped past, dark and pointed, its wings straight and true. Xander reached for Kelli's hand as a way to ground her in this reality.

"I can't believe it," Kelli finally breathed.

Charlie's eyes had filled with tears, too. "You'll have to forgive me. I'm something of a sentimentalist in my old age— always wearing my heart on my sleeve. I suppose when you get to a certain age, you want everything to feel big, enormous, and worthwhile. I am so grateful for all the events and all of the emotions in my life, just as I know my father was grateful for Marilyn."

Xander squeezed Kelli's hand still harder. Several tears trickled down her cheek.

"And what about the hotel?" Kelli whispered. "What did your father say about that?"

Charlie laughed at that. The motion was so abrupt that his eyes released tears.

"He never told me about the hotel," he finally admitted. "All that information he gave me, and never once did he mention it. But I suppose he told his lawyer. I received a call saying that someone was attempting to steal an old property of my father's out from under us. He showed me the deed and explained the circumstances. I told him, of course, to take legal action. And then— I did something I'd never done before. I opened my father's diary."

Kelli thought about both of them: opening up the wild

and secret thoughts of these long-dead family members, attempting to unravel the truth. It was a dramatic and emotional time for both of them.

"Which is how I figured out he'd planned to alter his will toward the end of his life," Charlie continued. He reached for the small dark blue book on the side table, cleared his throat, and began to read.

January 13, 1997

It is with a heavy heart that I remember the forties. I was overzealous in all things, a drunken fool with far too much money to throw around. I remember my brazen actions with closed eyes and a pounding heart— even as I know, very soon, this pounding heart will cease to pound, that soon, my eyes will not see. I think of Marilyn, who went off into the darkness far too soon. I hope I see her on the other side if only so I can apologize to her.

Money matters very little to me now, especially in my old age. It's a funny thing. I look at my children— at Charlie, Angela, Penelope, and Rick, and I feel that they've been my life's blessing, what it's all been for. My wife passed away two years ago, and I feel what it probably was that Robert felt when Marilyn left the world. I must follow after her. I cannot sleep in this bed without her.

But I've decided to alter my will. That old property on the cliffside has haunted my dreams since the hurricane threatened to take our lives back in 1943. I've felt the weight of that property since that day— daring myself to go back and do something with it, yet feeling that I could not set foot back on that island without having to reckon with the old version of myself. Sometimes, you really can't go backward in this life.

I've decided to leave the old property to Marilyn's family. She had two children, Wesley and Kerry, who've

A Vineyard Rebirth

gone on to have families of their own. The property belongs to them, as their hearts beat with a singular love for Martha's Vineyard, a love I wanted to but can never truly understand.

Charlie stopped reading and turned his eyes back toward Kelli's. "I suppose he never managed to translate this to his lawyer, as the lawyer was still under the impression that the property belongs to us, to the Peterson estate. But I'm the only one left. And I feel the passion behind my father's words. The property belongs to you now, Kelli, along with the rest of your family. Do with it what you will. I know it would make my father— and, God willing, Marilyn, incredibly happy. I hope they've found a way to mend their differences up in heaven."

In the silence that followed, Charlie shifted the book on his lap. The pages fluttered and released a very old photograph, which had been tucked tightly away in the back.

"Huh." He reached down and gripped the edge of the photograph, then flipped it to find the wedding photograph of Marilyn and James Peterson. "Wow. I've never seen this before."

He passed it toward Kelli and Xander, who gazed at it in disbelief.

"They are so young," Kelli breathed. "It's funny to see this now. As a forty-six-year-old woman, beyond so many of my life's mistakes, it's funny to see these people, these beautiful, beautiful people, mere months before they made some of the biggest, life-altering mistakes of their own life."

Charlie nodded. "They changed one another's lives. That's for certain. And in that way— they changed our lives. Without those two people in that photograph meeting and marrying, we wouldn't be here together."

"It's funny how life works, isn't it?" Kelli whispered.

"And it's funny how life doesn't work sometimes, too," Charlie returned with a wink. "I'm entirely grateful for that."

Chapter Twenty-Three

Marilyn's stomach swelled beneath her dress; the baby performed a little dance, shifting her feet percussively on the other side of her skin. Marilyn was reminded of once when she and Robert had been out on the sailboat and a whale had lifted toward the water, beckoning and waving beneath the surface. She'd felt the enormity of the ferocious ocean below, the suggestion that there was so much lurking beneath the surface that she nor anyone living above ground could possibly comprehend.

Marilyn's hand stretched over her stomach in response, as though the two of them could wave hello to one another. "Do you hear me, my little peanut?" she whispered, there at the front desk of the Sunrise Cove. "Everything will be so much better when you come out here and join us. Your father and I are waiting."

It had been six years since Marilyn had arrived on the Vineyard. In those six years, it seemed that everything in her life had flipped on its head. She now felt like a full-scale islander, as she'd married into one of the most important families on the island, with roots all the way back to the 1600s. Her family back in upstate New York was well taken care of; Robert had seen to that. There had even been discussion of their coming to the island eventually, although Marilyn felt hesitant. There was a freedom in the life she and Robert had built with one another; she no longer had to answer to the way things had been beforehand.

This wasn't to say the previous few years hadn't had their share of hardships. Both of Robert's parents had passed away unexpectedly, which had led to Marilyn and Robert taking over the Sunrise Cove Inn in their wake. Robert's eyes had grown shadowed with each death and the heaviness of the burden they'd left behind. It was difficult sometimes for Marilyn to draw up the image of that long-ago man, that man who'd caught her attention as she'd been latched alongside James, trapped in a prison of high-society wealth and his volatility.

She hadn't heard from James since his departure. Sometimes, she still awoke in the middle of the night, drenched in sweat as fear permeated through her. Her mind told her she was still trapped in that loveless marriage, that James awaited her downstairs and required her to be finely dressed with her hair done just perfect. When she awoke from these dreams, she found Robert's powerful arms wrapped around her; he whispered to her that he was there, that everything was all right. She never described the dreams to him. Often, the dreams slipped away from her as she calmed and fell against Robert, so grateful for the warmth of his body and his masculine scent and the scratchiness of his flannel pajamas.

Robert appeared now in the doorway of the Sunrise Cove. He'd been out back, chopping wood, and now he marched toward her, dropped his mouth over hers, and closed his eyes. He smelled like the woods, like the ocean, and she placed her hand over his chest and felt the thump-thump of his beating heart. How alive they were that they could bring another life into this world! It was beyond her wildest dreams.

"We're fully booked tonight," she told him when their kiss broke.

Robert beamed. "I think we'll have a little bonfire along the beach. Me and Rod plan to play guitar, do a few songs for the guests."

"The guests love when you perform." Marilyn beamed at her husband as her heart swelled. "And you know, I always had a thing for musicians."

Robert chuckled. His hand found hers, stretched over her stomach, and he pressed lightly against it, uniting the three of them.

"This is the last summer of just us, you know?" Robert breathed.

"We've had our fun," Marilyn returned. "Six years of it."

"Are you suggesting it's time to grow up?"

"Never," Marilyn returned. "In fact, I think we'll only grow backward. Appreciate this world the way children do. Relish in the sunset and the sunrise and the ocean and the breeze and the trees and the flowers. I never want to dismiss any of it."

Robert's eyes glowed. He lifted his hand and pressed it against her cheek. "What did I do to deserve you, Marilyn? I ask God above every day."

"I ask him that, too, my love."

* * *

Marilyn and Robert were in the midst of building a house about a mile away from the Sunrise Cove. For now, they stayed in a little cabin on the Sunrise Cove property, one so small that it reminded Marilyn of old books she'd read about families out on the prairie, running across the United States and taking claim of land along the way. She teased Robert about this often, pretending that they were on the Oregon Trail, headed west to seek their fortune.

"I'll have you in a good house one of these days," Robert said. He stood shirtless in their kitchen, with his suspenders wrapped around his broad shoulders.

Marilyn lay back against the kitchen counter so that her pregnant belly bulged between them.

"I have been meaning to tell you, Marilyn. Perhaps you don't know," Robert said, mocking a serious face. "You really need to tend to your figure. People have begun to talk."

Marilyn stuck out her tongue in response and then laughed as Robert rushed toward her and kissed her cheek, her forehead, her lips, and her neck. She marveled at the enormity of their happiness— knowing only that when the baby came, that same happiness would balloon perhaps twenty times its size.

"The only talking they did was about why we waited so long to have a baby," Marilyn said mischievously.

"I know. Must puzzle them to think that we were just too in love to bother with anyone else," Robert quipped.

It had been thrilling, that freedom: sailing expeditions and wild horseback rides and hikes that had traced them across the island and back again. They'd fallen into conversation with countless tourists from all walks of life and frequently stayed up till dawn, gazing into one another's eyes. It was time for the next portion of their journey together; Marilyn welcomed it with open arms, even as they said goodbye to the old ways.

"What do you think we should call our baby?" Marilyn whispered.

Robert's smile lightened. He pressed a strand of hair behind her ear, then said, "If it's a girl— like you keep telling me it is— then I think it's up to you to choose."

"And if it's a boy?"

Robert shrugged. "Still your choice. I'll call them whatever you like and give you two all the love I have in the world."

Chapter Twenty-Four

Kelli awoke in Xander's California King-sized bed the morning after meeting Charlie Peterson. She was alone, and from where she lay back, splayed beneath the comforter, she could hear the rush of water from the attached bathroom, where Xander showered. She burrowed herself deeper beneath the thousand-count sheets but laced her hand out toward the bedside table to again grip the old photograph of James and Marilyn Peterson, the doomed couple, which Charlie had given to her prior to her departure the previous night. When she'd initially resisted, he'd just said, "I won't be around much longer. I want you to have it. I want you to know that my father really loved her in his own way, even if he couldn't show it."

"How young you were, Marilyn," she whispered to the photograph of her grandmother.

Xander stepped out of the bathroom in a fluffy white robe. He sat at the edge of the bed and placed his hand over the mound in the comforter, where her thigh was. Her smile widened.

"How was your shower?"

"Just what I needed," he replied. He then glanced toward the window, where the view from the forty-third floor revealed a gray and somber morning, thick with fog and speckled with rain. "I wonder if you'd like to have breakfast in the city before we head back?"

Kelli lifted herself onto the fluffy pillows and allowed him to gently press his lips onto hers.

"I don't even know how I'll manage to get out of this bed," she told him. "I think that was the best sleep of my life."

"Yeah? Was it the bed? Or the company?" Xander asked with a cheeky grin.

Kelli laughed. "Is that a bit of that Manhattan arrogance peeking through? Already, this early in the morning?"

"I can't help it. I just want to know what you think of me," Xander teased. "I'm dying to know."

Kelli captured his hand and laced her fingers through it, there on the white shine of the comforter. Her smile faltered as the enormity of her brewing feelings came over her.

"Let's just say you have a lot to look forward to," she said finally.

Xander chuckled. "That sounds oddly scary."

"Maybe it is."

"All right. I'll prepare myself to be absolutely terrified," Xander returned.

* * *

Kelli and Xander spent the morning in Manhattan. They dined at an iconic brunch place a few blocks away from

Central Park, where they shared an overstuffed cheesy-everything-bagel, cut through the yolks of their eggs so that the yellow gooped out, and laughed about nonsensical issues, even talking about how they'd been as children.

"I was a skinny kid, to say the least," Xander explained as he twirled his fork over the top of his egg. "Always apt to get into a fight over something stupid. But I had passion, and I guess I attribute the rest of my life to that passion."

Kelli beamed at him as the server poured her another cup of coffee. "I can't believe I get to take you back to the Vineyard with me."

"Are you kidding? It's really the only place I want to be," Xander admitted as he leaned forward. "Already, the city air is getting to me. Take me to the seaside, Kelli! I need that sweet, healing air!"

During his performance, the server approached to ask if they needed anything else. She ogled Xander with confusion as Kelli burst into laughter.

"Sorry for his outburst," Kelli said. "He isn't very good in public spaces. Always carrying on like this."

Xander winked as the server marched away, clearly annoyed.

"I can't take you anywhere," Kelli affirmed.

"That's a good thing because, for the next year or two, it's going to be all Cliffside Overlook Hotel, all the time." Xander furrowed his brow, then added, "I want to take a really good look at those blueprints and see if we can make them a reality again. Such good luck that you found them. We can bring the history of the old hotel to life. Maybe we can even have a grand opening party with an old 1940s theme, as though the place was never destroyed."

"Sounds like a good way to drudge up old ghosts," Kelli said.

"I suppose, in a way, we're calling them back," Xander admitted. "But the island is filled with ghosts, I think. You can feel it when you're walking the trails or along the beach. I sat on the docks recently as the boats creaked in the darkness. I swear, it could have been any other time, in any other era. Men and women have been sailing into the waters surrounding Martha's Vineyard for centuries. We're a part of such a beautiful, long-standing tradition."

"And maybe we'll someday be the island's ghosts ourselves," Kelli returned.

Xander laughed even as his eyes grew broad. "You're probably right about that, Kelli. If all things go to plan, we can haunt this Overlook Hotel together."

Kelli giggled. "You're ridiculous; you know that?"

"I hope so. It seems to me that being ridiculous is the only way to live," Xander said.

They returned to Xander's convertible, where Kelli helped him lift the top and latch it safely in place, as the rain hadn't cut out that morning. Inside the vehicle, Kelli felt safe and cocooned. Xander told her she could lay back on the seat if she wanted to and grab some shut-eye, but she resisted. "I don't want to leave you alone," she murmured, even as her eyes grew hazy with the gray light outside and the fatigue after the dramatic trip.

The drive back to the Vineyard was similarly warm and nourishing as Kelli and Xander swapped stories and grew increasingly excited about the weeks ahead. They knew they needed to get as much done on the exterior of the Overlook Hotel before the winter months, as winter on the Vineyard could be frighteningly chilly and thick with snow.

When they reached Woods Hole, Xander drove the convertible into the belly of the ferry and turned off the engine. Kelli leaped out to stretch her legs. Xander followed her upstairs, where they purchased wine and a beer, respectively, and stood against the barrier between them and the rushing waters below. For whatever reason, Kelli felt as though her words were at a great distance from her, and she allowed the silence to unfurl itself, growing stronger and more powerful as they steamed toward the island. She placed her head on Xander's chest and listened to the banging of his heart as they went. Someday soon, maybe, she would describe the level of safety she felt around him— and what a great contrast that was to her previous life with Mike. But for now, she would just enjoy it.

When they arrived on the island, Kelli dialed her mother's number. To her surprise, it rang a few times before going to voicemail.

"No answer?" Xander asked. He slid deeper into the driver's seat and latched his seatbelt.

"Nothing. Let me try again." Again, the phone blared several times without an answer. Kelli balked, then lifted her eyes to the gray light of the early afternoon. Suddenly, the phone rang— this time with Lexi's name.

"Mom! Hey! I saw you were calling Grandma's phone." Lexi sounded out of breath.

"Hey, honey. Are you all right?"

Xander cast Kelli a look of confusion.

"Um. Kind of. Actually, do you mind coming by the boutique? I called Grandma for back-up, but even that isn't enough."

Kelli had never seen the boutique with more than two or three customers. "Of course, honey. I'll be right there?"

But already, Lexi had returned to the store and its apparent chaos. Kelli pressed the END button and instructed Xander where to drive.

"Ah, right. Your other business."

"My daughter has really been picking up the slack there," Kelli said with a soft smile. "I've gone in and out and helped with inventory, but she's really proven herself to me this summer. I'm really proud of her."

Just as Lexi had said, the boutique was overblown with tourists. There was a line of ten people snaking around the side, and within, fifteen people had crammed themselves, hunting through the vast array of beautiful blouses, skirts, dresses, shoes, and old hats. The dressing rooms were full, and there was a long wait line at the counter, where Lexi had put her Grandma Kerry to work. Kerry furrowed her brow as she selected each button, ringing up each item and declaring the price to each customer. Her normally perfect hair was frazzled, as though she'd run her fingers through it too many times. Lexi was off in the corner, putting away tossed-aside items from the dressing room as quickly as she could. Her eyes were enormous with panic, but her smile said it all: she was enjoying this success.

"Let me just jump in there and help out for a bit, all right?" she told Xander just as she flung herself into the chaos. She passed by her mother and called, "Thank you for the help, Mom!" just before she joined Lexi in putting things away, tidying the store, and answering customer questions. Throughout, she was reminded that this, in fact, had been her passion project, not real estate, and she was so grateful that Lexi had been able to keep her baby afloat. She would have flung her arms around her daughter if not for the hubbub of people, all hungry for their gorgeous vintage and designer collections.

"What brought everyone in today, anyway?" she called to Lexi during a small break in people.

Lexi laughed. "Remember that wedding Charlotte put on last year?"

"How could I forget?" The iconic wedding of the century between actress Ursula Pennington and her basketball player husband had nearly destroyed her younger sister's psyche.

"Well, Ursula came back to the island for a visit. Nostalgia for her wedding or something, I guess. She was in yesterday and put everything on social media. She went crazy for our stuff, advertising us everywhere. After that, the store has been stuffed to the gills," Lexi explained.

Lexi, Kelli, and Kerry became like a well-oiled machine as they worked over the next hour. Kelli's heart grew ten sizes, it seemed like, as she watched her mother pour her love into her passion project. For years, Kerry had pretended not to understand the boutique, wondering why Kelli didn't just give it all to the real estate business. Perhaps this was proof that she finally understood it.

Finally, at five p.m., Lexi herself flipped the sign from OPEN to CLOSED. She then gasped and fell to the ground as Kerry started a slow clap. Kelli laughed aloud at the chaos of the store, which looked as though it had been picked over by vultures.

"What were our sales today?" Lexi asked her grandmother excitedly.

Kerry shuffled her way through the computer until

she drew up a number. "Nine thousand dollars," Kerry whispered and then whistled. "Damn, I was in the wrong business."

Kelli flew an arm around Lexi's shoulder and held her tightly against her. Her eyes were alight. She then glanced toward her phone, where Xander had texted to say he'd headed back to his place for the rest of the day, but to let him know if she needed him in any respect.

Right then, all she needed was her family.

"I have such a story for the two of you," Kelli said finally.

They sat in a circle on the floor of the boutique as Kelli explained everything. Lexi played soft music on her Bluetooth speaker as Kerry gazed down at the photograph of her mother and the man she'd long-ago divorced. Her eyes were rimmed red with tears.

"I can't believe this," she whispered. "Look at how young she was. She didn't have me until six years after this. Her marriage to James must have felt like such a long-ago memory."

"Charlie Peterson is one of James Peterson's four children and the only remaining one alive," Kelli explained. "He spoke about his father much differently than I've been led to think about him. I think he regretted the way he treated Grandma and actually learned from his mistakes."

"Wow." Kerry sniffed as she placed the photo back in Kelli's outstretched palm. "I'm sorry. I just feel speechless. I've always been so curious about my mother. And since the other night, I've pored over her diary even more, getting a better sense of her. Do you want to hear a funny entry?"

Kelli and Lexi both nodded, excited. Kerry leafed

through her purse to draw out the old diary. She cleared her throat and then began to read.

February 14, 1944

I love Robert. I've never loved anyone more than him in all my life.

But I've come to the unfortunate realization that he snores like a train.

What's to be done? I suppose nothing in this life is perfect.

But I suppose as I love him so fiercely, I will find a way to sleep through the night.

At this, Kelli and Lexi howled with laughter. Kerry chuckled and snapped the book closed.

"That's it?" Lexi asked. "That's all she wrote on Valentine's Day of 1944?"

"I suppose that's all that was on her mind that day," Kerry affirmed. "But the rest of the diary is so beautiful. I love her descriptions of my Sheridan Grandparents and how kind they were to her when she first arrived. She talks about conversations she had with my grandmother and about little tasks she helped her with around the Sunrise Cove. I can remember helping my mother with those same tasks. It makes me feel like I belong to this great line of women— even though these women left this earth much too soon."

"We're here in their wake," Kelli said softly. "I feel them in everything. Xander told me today that he thinks the island is filled with ghosts. I think I agree with him."

"We carry them within us," Kerry offered. "I can see my mother and my grandmother in both of your faces. I can feel my mother and father's hard work in the way we operated the boutique only just this afternoon. We are the products of multiple generations of hard-working, loyal, and loving people. How grateful I am for that."

*　*　*

Three weeks later, when the initial construction for the next generation of the Aquinnah Cliffside Overlook Hotel began, the entire Montgomery-Sheridan clan stood near the cliff's edge and watched as Kelli and Xander sliced a long red ribbon in celebration of the moment. Kerry and Wes stood off to the side with their hands latched together, then took equal time at the microphone, explaining what it meant to them to know that the place where their mother and father had met would one day tower over the cliffside once more.

"We are given such a finite amount of time on this earth," Kerry said as her eyes swirled with so much emotion. "My mother and father were taken much too soon. But I feel them here in the air and in the water and in the trees. I can't wait to close my eyes within the new construction of the Overlook Hotel and feel the intrigue and excitement that my mother felt when she first spotted the love of her life. On the day they met, all of Martha's Vineyard's future changed for the better. None of us in the Montgomery and Sheridan families would be here if it weren't for them." She then lifted her eyes toward the glistening clouds above and splayed out a hand. "If you can hear us, Mom and Dad, we love you. And we've kept up the love you had for one another in all things. Just as you wanted us to do."

Coming Next

Next in the series

Other Books by Katie

The Vineyard Sunset Series

Secrets of Mackinac Island Series

Sisters of Edgartown Series

A Katama Bay Series

A Mount Desert Island Series

A Nantucket Sunset Series

Made in United States
North Haven, CT
25 November 2024